2
Peo|

The Way We Loved

Ambition Took Her Away
Pride Kept Him There
Fate Brought Them Back Together

TINLEY BLAKE

THE WAY WE LOVED

TINLEY BLAKE

Copyright © 2019 by Tinley Blake

All rights reserved. Neither this book, nor any portion thereof, may be reproduced or used in any manner whatsoever without the express written permission of the publisher except for the use of brief quotations in a book review.

Printed in the United States of America

First Printing, 2019

www.tinleyblake.com

For Riley

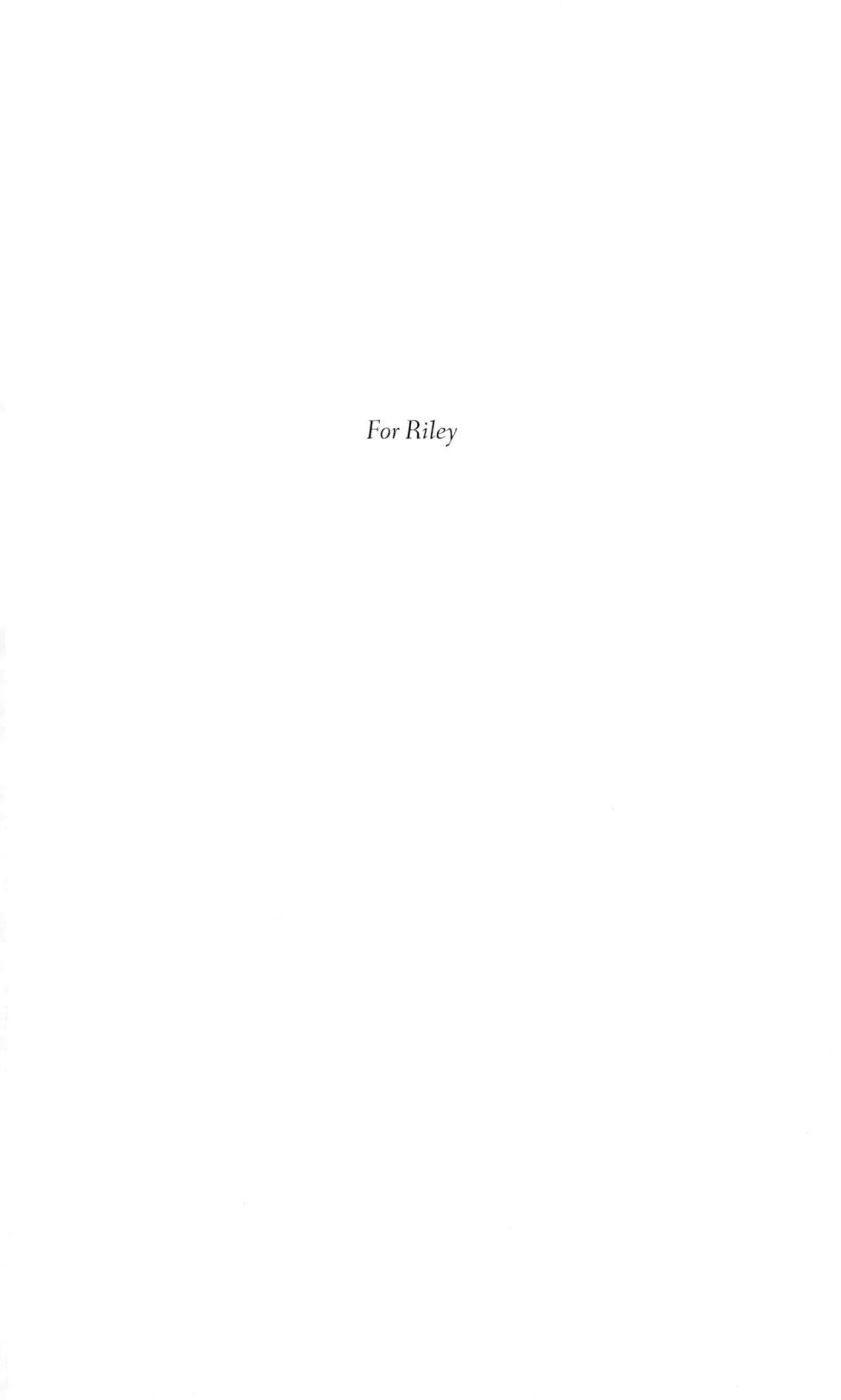

TABLE OF CONTENTS

The Way We Loved	1
Chapter 1	3
Chapter 2	13
Chapter 3	23
Chapter 4	31
Chapter 5	41
Chapter 6	49
Chapter 7	55
Chapter 8	63
Chapter 9	71
Chapter 10	81
Chapter 11	87
Chapter 12	93
Chapter 13	99
Chapter 14	103
Chapter 15	107
Chapter 16	119
Chapter 17	123
Chapter 18	129
Chapter 19	135
Chapter 20	139
Chapter 21	143
Chapter 22	149
Chapter 23	153
Chapter 24	159
Chapter 25	163
Chapter 26	167
Chapter 27	175
Chapter 28	183
Chapter 29	189
Chapter 30	197

Chapter 31	205
Chapter 32	211
Chapter 33	221
Chapter 34	229
Chapter 35	239
Chapter 36	247
Chapter 37	253
Chapter 38	259
Chapter 39	267
Chapter 40	273
Chapter 41	277
Chapter 42	281
Epilogue	287
Acknowledgements	295
About Tinley	299
Author Works	301

The stars were blacked out the night you left
It was an omen of things to come
Your departure left me bereft
And stole my happy ever after
There will be no one but you
No one will ever come close
This is the story of us
And of
The way we loved

-K. Moore

CHAPTER ONE

#freshstart

Blake

MY FEET HATE ME.

To be fair, I don't blame them. I shove them into tiny holes with high arches and then force them to support me for hours on end. Which they do, without fail, until today. Today, the most important day of my career, of my life, they protest.

Halfway through the podcast, I can't stand it anymore. I press a toed heel against the back of the other, wedging my foot out. They fall to the ground with a thump, one after the other. I can't concentrate on anything with my toes screaming at me. Tony, the producer, raises his dark brow. I shrug and read back over my lines.

Six years ago, I started the *Fresh Start* morning podcast. It focuses on real-life women, men, and children and how we can help each other become the best versions of ourselves. Each day, I wake at the crack of dawn and go live, answering questions submitted by listeners or touching on topics no one else cares to broach. Each day, the number of people I reach grows.

In the beginning, I couldn't take a photo without screwing something up. There was a lot of trial and error in the early days of my Instagram account. It took me a month before I gained a hundred followers. My Facebook account contained thirty-seven friends. It's maxed out at five thousand now.

But what started as a dream and an Instagram page morphed into multimillions of followers and unlimited open doors. I wanted to step through every single one of them and take my place on stage. To shout from every rooftop and scream down every alley.

You can do this. You can do anything. Take today and make a Fresh Start.

Today was the next step. When I first received the call about doing this segment, the call went to my voicemail. I listened to that voicemail over and over at least twenty times before jumping on the kitchen counter, shaking my fists in the air, and screaming at the top of my lungs.

It wasn't every day you got noticed by Carl Brighton, CEO of Brighton Industries, the largest and most well-respected platform in LA. And they wanted me. Or at least, they thought they did.

The call was an audition of sorts. Carl himself wanted me to come to LA as a guest on his podcast and speak about relationships. His focus at the moment was on particular types like marriage and the ways to be successful in creating a healthy relationship. I had already done a similar screening on my channel, which went over well, so I broke out my notebooks and started brainstorming. If Carl wanted to put me on stage, by God, I'd give him the show of his life.

If only I had worn socks, then maybe my feet wouldn't interject with cries of pain during every thought I attempted to have. The podcast was meant to be an hour long. We lost track of the time and ended up going over by fifteen minutes. I call that a win. Any time you're so caught up in something that time passes without notice is time well spent. Carl himself thanked me when I finished.

"Wonderful work today, Miss Smith."

"Thanks for having me. I look forward to the possibility of working together in the future."

"You can count on it," he says, brushing a hand against my lower back. "Maybe next time you're out, I'll have my secretary schedule lunch, or better yet, dinner." Carl Brighton doesn't seem like the type of man to be told no about anything, and even if I wasn't dying for the opportunity to pick his brain, I wouldn't deny him lunch. Only a fool would. The man is a bucket of knowledge. An overflowing bucket, and I am parched.

"I look forward to returning. You've been an inspiration for years. I hope to one day achieve a percentage of what you have." My voice doesn't sound like my own. It's risen several octaves and it's taking everything I have to not jump up and down like a starstruck teenager.

"With your tenacity, I'm sure you will continue to climb the ladder of success, Miss Smith." He opens the door leading to the street. "Until next time."

One day, I hope to see women succeed in this world without men tearing them down and using them for stepping-stones on their path to success. Some of the most brilliant people I have ever met were women. One of my favorite authors included. She hates all men, and the longer I'm in this business, the more I see why, but then I meet someone like Carl and the tiny flame of hope reignites within my soul. We can work together. It doesn't have to be a competition, men against women. We can support one another and push each other to succeed.

The drive to the airport is short, even with traffic. Everything I brought out with me is tucked neatly into my rolling suitcase that doubles as my briefcase. Over the years, I've learned to pack lightly and efficiently, which allows me to skip the lines at check-in. At the gate, I scroll through my phone, adding photos to my favorites folder for future posts while I wait for my group to be called. The entire flight takes less time than security at LAX.

Just landed. I text Brad while the plane taxis on the runway. Young couples stand before the light dings, opening overhead bins and pulling their suitcases free. A child cries at the front of the plane, irritated and ready to run. I understand, kiddo. I hate sitting here too, but still, I sit and wait. As soon as the plane doors open, the aisle fills with bodies. It's a rushed, chaotic affair to exit the plane. I'm one of the last to stand, preferring to wait for the crowd to clear rather than fight my way through it.

Brad and I haven't spoken since this morning before I went live. At the time, I'd planned to stay in LA and sightsee a little before heading back home, but the segment this morning, coupled with Carl Brighton's comments on marriage, had me missing him. Brad would never assume that I could only succeed by climbing the ladder, an innuendo for sleeping my way to the top, even if he was upset with me. Things had been weird between us since he proposed, and a lot of that had to do with me, but he supports me and believes in my dreams. It's hard to agree to spend forever with someone when you aren't sure what course your own life is going to take, but we've been dating for three years and he felt it was time to solidify our futures.

I could have waited another three years. The thought of planning a wedding right now terrifies me. My career is my number-one priority. I don't want to take any time away from that. Brad has his future planned out in ways that often remind me of sixth-grade little girls. He wants the wife, the nice house, the required one or two kids, and summer vacations in the same spot every year. He wants to put down roots and start traditions. I want those things too, just not at this point in my life.

When he doesn't text back, I schedule an Uber and make my way to the pickup location inside the airport parking garage, then I sit and wait for the white Ford Fusion to pull in.

Today's topic of marriage and the ways to put your best foot forward in every relationship made me realize I've been pulling away from Brad. He's been an amazing support for me while navigating the business world and has stood by me while I was finding my way and growing my brand. He hasn't minded my long hours or the fact that half the time, I forget our dinner dates. Some days, I wonder why he stays. His life would be a lot simpler without my forgetfulness.

I look up his favorite Thai restaurant and place an online order and then update my route for Uber, smiling to myself. I would surprise him today with food and then spend all night making up for my distance.

It's going to be great. I text him when I'm almost home.
I've missed you.

His car is in the driveway. I see it as soon as my Uber driver turns on Cherry Street. I check my phone once more before thanking my driver and climbing from the backseat. The sun is making its descent for the evening. Pinks, purples, oranges, and reds streak across the horizon, casting a golden glaze on the hood of this red Camaro. I run my fingers along it on my way to the front door. He keeps it so clean you can't even see my print.

Brad's shirt is on the floor just inside the entry. It's the first thing I see when I step across the threshold. Followed by his belt at the bottom of the stairs. I climb them dazedly, unable to process what I'm seeing. My eyes blink rapidly, but with every open and close, the items remain, scattered like pieces of a jigsaw puzzle that I can't connect. I step around a pair of four-inch black heels before reaching my bedroom door. My hands are trembling so badly I can't grasp the door handle.

I push the door open with my foot, my heart beating so hard I worry it will jump out of my chest. I can't hear past the *thump, thump, thump* of it. I fight the urge to squeeze my eyes shut, to block out the scene before me. My stomach sours. I can taste the acid in the back of my throat.

The room is empty.

In the corner next to my bed is a lime green chair I bought at a yard sale two years ago for five dollars. It doesn't match any of my décor, but I love it. That chair is my catch-all for clothes when I'm trying to find something to wear. I cleaned it off before I left, hanging everything back in the closet nice and neatly. I wanted to come home to a clean space so I could unwind and relax from the plane ride. It was a ritual of mine.

There's a black dress laid across it now.

My black dress.

I hear him now, in the bathroom, and take the four steps

across the room on silent tiptoes. Outside the door, I pause. My whole body is shaking with the effort it takes to move. My eyes burn, unshed tears fighting to fall. I pull in a breath through my nose and hold it for the span of three thumps of my heart before blowing it out between clenched teeth.

There is no denying what I will see when I open the door. I know because I can hear them now, laughing and grunting. The sound of flesh hitting flesh. She moans and calls out his name in a rushed breath, the way you do right before losing yourself to all thought.

I know because I recognize the black dress tossed across my favorite lime green chair in the corner of my bedroom. The silky black dress I'd loaned to my best friend the night before I left.

She had a hot date with a guy she was seeing. I hadn't met him yet, or at least didn't know I had. It would appear that I was engaged to him.

I can't open the door. There are a few images you don't want seared into your mind. At the top of my list was seeing the two people I should be able to count on most betraying me. Not exactly knowing how to react, I stand there, momentarily lost and searching for answers that are nowhere to be found. A guttural moan brings me from my thoughts, and I turn to toss the bag of food on the bed. It spills open and one of the lids comes free, covering my white comforter with the spicy Thai chicken and rice. It's out of the bag. Pun intended.

The engagement ring comes off with remarkable ease, and I place it on the table by the front door and take a deep breath. My chest feels lighter. The ceramic bowl clinks as I grab my keys, and I stop. I should be upset. I should be crying my eyes out, overwhelmed and inconsolable. But I'm not.

All I feel is relief.

Have your things out by morning.

You can keep the dress.

The first text I send to Brad. The second to Cindy. Then I block them both and back out of the drive. It doesn't make any sense to leave the house I am paying for, but it's the last place I want to be. I don't know if I will ever want to be there again. I still haven't been back to my mother's house, and I lost her over a decade ago. When I feel pain, I connect it to an object and then avoid that object forever. Plus, I only bought the place to placate Brad for a little longer in an effort to avoid the wedding talk. It worked for a year.

I drive with no destination in mind. Maybe I'm in shock. I hold one hand up to check whether it's shaking as badly as I feel like I am, but it's steady.

In control.

Until it's not.

As I drive, the scenario replays over and over in my mind. There are a hundred things I'd do differently if given the chance. It was a telling sign for our relationship that my first reaction to his betrayal was relief, but as I drive with no destination in mind, relief quickly morphs into anger. I might have been relieved to get out of the predicament that was our future marriage, but he was the one who wanted it to begin with. So why would he throw the potential of that perfect white-fence life with me away—with Cindy, of all people? *Why would he do that? How could he do that?*

A part of me wants to blame myself for this. I've been distant and self involved. I could have made more time for him. At the very least, I should have shown him more attention.

Shoulda. Coulda. Woulda.

Great. Now I sound like a country song.

The more I think about their betrayal, the angrier I become. Regardless of where I was mentally, I still cared for Brad. I may have been finding it hard to come to grips with the whole marriage thing, but I was coming around. So why would he risk it all for a quick lay? Why would he throw our future away?

The logical part of my brain knows this all falls on him. Brad chose this, and he knew what he was doing when he did it. What's worse is he knew I would find out. I'm a nosy person. I dig for shit that isn't even there. If I have a hunch something is off, then I'm worse than a hound treeing a squirrel. I won't stop until I figure out what is triggering my obsessiveness.

Today, I gave the best speech of my life about love, trust, commitment, and how to create a lasting, healthy relationship. All the while, my own relationship was complete and total trash. I'm a liar. A fraud. I'm your sweet Aunt Sally who goes to church Sunday and swears by Jesus, cursing sinners to the brink of hell, but then goes home Monday through Friday and lives like the Devil's mistress. I have no business teaching other people how to be better versions of themselves. I can't even keep my own life together.

"So much for having a great day," I mumble, turning into the hotel. "And my damn feet still hurt."

CHAPTER TWO

#goinghome

Blake

AN AMETHYST TINT invades the late summer sky as I crest Highway 77. My windows are rolled down, and the sweet fragrance of honeysuckles saturates my senses. The sound of humming locusts fills the air. Summer is fading and with it the long, endless days.

Arriving back in my hometown is similar to finding an old sweatshirt from college and curling up in front of a warm fire with a bottle of wine. I wasn't expecting the familiarity, but I'm so glad for it.

The air smells fresher, cleaner than the stuff back west. My lungs fill with it, and for the first time since catching my fiancé cheating, the tightness in my chest eases. I can breathe.

The drive from Arizona to Alabama is long, a fact reinforced by driving 1670 straight miles. Almost thirty hours in my Malibu, packed to the brim with whatever I couldn't stand to leave with the movers. I labeled all the items I wanted to keep, and Brad could have the rest. His taste had never lined up with mine, anyway, and the last thing I wanted was a room full of his crap. The rest of my belongings would be here in three weeks as long as the moving company didn't run into any hiccups along the way.

Expect the best. Prepare for the worst.

One of my mother's favorite sayings. I thought of her more on this trip than all the days of the last year combined. It seems fitting that thoughts of her follow me back into town, considering it was her memory that had chased me out of here to begin with.

I can't help but wonder if she were alive, would she be disappointed in me? I've made a real muck of things.

Brad made his grand appearance the night before I hit the road. It was the first time I had seen him since that fateful day almost three months prior, although I guess technically, I didn't see him that day, either. The morning after my drunken stay at the hotel, I returned home, and he was gone along with all of his clothes and toiletries. My schedule at the time had been set in stone, so for the next couple of months, I traveled, giving speeches and trying to come to grips with my new normal. I had lost something, and I didn't know how to get it back.

Brad appeared surprised to see the house packed up, but he didn't comment on it and I was glad. I didn't want him to know I was going back to my hometown—didn't want him under the impression that I was tucking tail and running away because of him. I never let an opportunity to tell him how much I hated Alabama go to waste. How happy I was to be gone. Now look at me. Don't get me wrong. I was still fuming at the betrayal, and thinking his name made me want to puke, but I wasn't going back home because of him.

I need to come to terms with the mess my life has turned into, and I didn't know how to do that in the house that reminded me of how screwed up it was. A house I never wanted to begin with in a city I'd rather not live in. At my core, I thought I was on a good path. I thought I was doing well. If someone had asked me while doing the podcast how to handle a cheating spouse, I would have spat out ten thousand answers, all of them centered on forgiving and how to grow from it, but when I walked in that door, all of that went out the window. I couldn't talk flowers and rainbows and mending broken bridges when all I wanted to do was set fire to the whole place. Hell, if someone came to me right now and said the things I know I would have, I would be hard pressed to not slap them. Who the hell did I think I was, telling women and men that their pain wasn't justified, that they should let it all go? A joke, that's who I was.

Fresh Start was left in the capable hands of my assistant with strict instructions to contact me daily with any questions or concerns. She ran the place already. The only difference now would be that instead of seeing me daily, she'd need to call me. Sitting in the floor of the guest bedroom, I'd stuffed my face with food and scheduled a month's worth of Instagram and Facebook posts. Shelly, my assistant, emailed any prior event coordinators to reschedule, or in the event they didn't want to, cancel. For the first time in six years, I was taking a break and focusing on what I needed. One day, I planned to pick it all back up, but I couldn't in good faith do so until I had the scrambled mess of thoughts swarming like vultures around a carcass straightened out first.

I'd been toying with the idea of taking a vacation for a few months. Well, since catching Brad, but I didn't want to lie on a beach and listen to waves wash ashore. I needed to work. I just didn't want to be the face of change right now. I was tired of showing up on stage and putting on a smile that I didn't feel. Even the thought of lunch with Carl couldn't break me out of my sullen mood. The only thing that helped was visiting the shelter. I had started volunteering there a few years ago. It was more than philanthropic work for me. The animals were a balm that eased my mind and gave me a getaway from my busy schedule. They were my family. Another thing that Brad didn't understand. His idea of helping others was tossing change in a bucket, and even that was stretching it for him.

What had begun as menial work that didn't require too much thinking had quickly turned into one of my most sacred reprieves. Especially the horses. Before volunteering at the shelter, I hadn't seen or touched a horse in the years since leaving home. Now, I didn't go a week without them.

The shrill ring of my cell breaks me out of my inner thoughts. I fish around in my purse with one hand while keeping my eyes on the road and then abandon the search altogether and press the car's Bluetooth button.

"Hello?" My fingers lift the control buttons, rolling the windows back up one and a time, until I can hear more than the wind in my ears.

"What's up, Sunshine? You make it in yet?" Beau's country drawl, heightened after a long day and lack of sleep, fills my car speakers. When I spoke to him this morning, he filled me in on part of his daily routine. It made my daily schedule look like kindergarten recess.

"I just passed Old Man Pete's." Glancing back, I watch the old ruin fade in my rearview mirror.

"Well, hot damn, you're 'bout here. I got the room all cleaned out and had Greg come by and spray for critters, just in case. Honk when you pull up and I'll come help carry your stuff upstairs."

"Okay, sounds good. I'll see you in five." I press the *End* button on my dash, disconnecting from the call.

Beau and I have been friends since grade school. Along with Calvin, who I tried not to think about right now. Calvin and I had left things unfinished when I left town, and I still didn't know how to handle seeing him again. It had been eleven years since I last saw him or spoke to him. My leaving hurt him more than either of us expected it to. I'm almost positive Cal hasn't forgiven me for it.

Over the years, Beau and I stayed in touch. He followed my career and my life. Any time I had a big win, I could count on a package from home filled with berry jams and clippings from the local newspaper. I loved getting them. Not only because I knew he was keeping up with me, but also because they reminded me of home, of where I came from and how far I had made it.

Look at me now. Back in Greentown, Alabama, the place I ran from as fast I could the moment I turned eighteen. I hadn't looked back in all that time. Funny that now, it's the only place that feels safe.

I pull up to Beau's plantation-inspired home and honk twice.

It's strange how fate works, sometimes. I was about

halfway through the mini fridge in the hotel the night I caught Brad when Beau called. I tried to ignore the call, but in my intoxicated state, I pressed the green *Accept* button instead of the red *Decline*. It took less than twenty seconds before I unloaded on Beau. Most days, I'm more of a suffer in silence type of person, but that night, I needed to vent and he let me. When I finished, he told me to pack my shit and come home.

I had a dozen reasons why I couldn't, why it was a bad idea. He'd countered each one of them until the only one left was Calvin.

He will get over it. Don't worry about him. You need this.

He was right. I needed it, and if Calvin couldn't get over it, then screw him. Every day since that call, he has checked up on me, and every time, he asks when I plan to come. Of course, we both know part of his annoying pushiness has to do with the fact that he needs help too.

I've got one foot on solid ground and the other hovering above the driver's floorboard when Beau sweeps me up in his arms, pulling me the rest of the way out. My feet dangle inches off the ground. He squeezes me, and my back cracks in ten different places. I wrap my arms around his neck and breathe in the intoxicating scent of home.

"Fucking hell, Blake, it's been too long." He sets me on my feet and takes a step back. "Shit, you look like you got run over by a garbage truck."

I slap his chest. "Screw you, Beau. I told you I drove straight through." And doesn't he know you're never supposed to tell a girl she looks like hell? Men. I hate them all.

"Yeah, but you know you can brush your hair and drive at the same time," he says, dodging my striking hand.

"Shut up and help me carry this stuff inside so I can shower. *Asshole*," I mumble under my breath.

"I heard that."

Well, I certainly hope so. "Listen, I really appreciate you letting me stay here, Beau, "I say, looking around the converted apartment above his garage. "I couldn't . . . I didn't . . ." My words trail off and my throat constricts upon thinking about the home I grew up in with my mom. It's been here, abandoned by me all those years ago. I'm not ready to deal with it yet, just like I'm not ready to deal with my house in Arizona.

"It's not a problem. I'm here for as long as you need."

It takes three trips each before we get it all inside the small apartment above his garage. Eyeballing the stools around the counter, I contemplate sitting for a minute but decide on a shower instead. I really do stink.

"I'll be right back. Why don't you go grab us a couple of beers and meet me back here in twenty?" I say, taking a step toward the bathroom.

"Sure thing, Boss." Beau salutes on his way out the door.

Shaking my head, I go to scrub off a couple of layers of filth. It really does feel good to be back here even though I've just arrived. It's kinda like stopping by Grandma's after church on Sunday and falling asleep on the couch. There is a calmness or comfort in the known. This is my hometown and nothing like the big cities I was accustomed to spending time in. It was a simpler place. Not that people in Alabama didn't work hard. I'd be willing to bet half of my savings there were a few city slickers, Brad included, who wouldn't last a day in the South doing manual labor. It would damn well be funny to see his ass try.

There was less rush, less hustle here. People didn't mind stopping in the street to catch up with a friend they missed at

Sunday service. If a family was having a hard time, the whole town knew about it, but they also showed up with dinner and extra clothes their kids had outgrown. I'd never seen anyone in the city do that. The bigger cities were full of people, full of noise, full of life, but they lacked the simpler things. The things that made a place home.

It was a good idea, coming back here. The reasons I left no longer held power over me. I had healed and was too damn busy to realize it.

CHAPTER THREE

#fuckinghell

Calvin

WARM PINK and gold tendrils of light peek across the pasture line as I pull up at the ranch. I'm early, but since we had new help coming in this morning, I wanted to make sure I showed up before they did.

The kitchen light is on in Beau's, which means he's up and coffee is brewing. Gravel crunches under my feet, drowning out the wistful crow of Red, the ranch rooster. Frogs croak in the distance, competing with the playful chatter of the birds until Neo chases after them, barking.

Her laughter echoes through the morning air as soon as I step on the porch. Sweet, soft and tinkling. I've heard it every night for the last eleven years in my dreams. My mind can't process why I hear it now, but my legs don't seem to care either way. They carry me forward, searching, aching. My arms reach out and open the door without my deciding to do so.

In the next breath, she is standing in front of me and I'm drowning. She hasn't changed at all, and yet, everything has changed. Her honey brown eyes flit back and forth between me and Beau, who grabs another cup and fills it before passing it my way. I take it from him, my arms and hands continuing to perform outside of my awareness.

"You're early," he comments casually. Can't he see I'm losing my mind here? Either I'm going crazy or Blakelynn Smith is standing in front of me wearing a slip of a grin and the sexiest jeans I've ever seen on a woman.

I nod, still unable to force words out. She holds me captive with her gaze, her eyes scanning my face, searching, seeking. I need her to release me.

"Well, this has been fun. Blake, you ready to go meet the horses?" Beau asks, and Blake nods, pulling her gaze from mine. I have control of my body again, not that I know what to do with it. They pass by me on the way out the door, the smell of her lilac perfume snaking around and choking me with memories long since passed. I stand there for a moment staring at the empty pot, a mug of hot coffee in my hand, and try to understand what just happened. More importantly, why the hell was my Blake standing in Beau's kitchen at . . . I glance at the clock . . . 5:23 in the morning?

They're halfway to the barn when I walk out the door. My pulse rages, my heart beating wildly in my ears.

"Beau." He stops and turns back toward me. I watch his hand lift and touch her back, his other pointing to the barn. She takes a step forward, followed by another, without glancing back. I close the distance between Beau and me.

"Listen, I know this is hard . . ." he starts. I don't let him finish. My mind has latched onto the image of his hand brushing against her back.

Natural. Comfortable.

I haven't seen Blakelynn Smith in over ten years, and until a few moments ago, was under the impression that he hasn't either, but that touch leads me to believe I was wrong. So fucking wrong. I can't think straight. My brain and heart war with each other, one telling me there is no way Beau would hook up with Blake, behind my back or otherwise. He's my best friend. A brother to me. We've been through hell together and managed to pull ourselves back out of the fiery pits a time or two. Together. He knows what she meant to me. He wouldn't cross that line.

The other keeps revisiting the flash of his hand on her shoulder. Her standing in his kitchen, a slight, shy smile on her face. The fact that I had no knowledge of her coming here or why.

My heart wants to believe Beau is the friend I know him to be, but my mind deals with facts, and the glaring fact of the matter is that Blake is here and Beau didn't tell me.

I shove him hard. He stumbles back a few steps, holding his hands up in surrender. "Calvin, calm the hell down."

I shove him again. "What the hell was that? What the hell is she doing here in your house?" I grind the words out, the scene replaying over and over.

I push his shoulders again, but this time, he doesn't move. His hands push back against me. "You need to stop. You don't want this."

He's wrong. This is exactly what I want. I need this. My arm darts out, my swing hitting him squarely in the jaw. "How could you do this? You, of all fucking people." I want to hit him again and again, but he won't fight me back. Instead, he steps to the side, avoiding me when I take a step toward him, my fist balled, my pulse still screaming in my ears to do something. Anything.

"It's not like that, and fuck you for even thinking it." A red blush creeps up his face. His anger is showing, even if he refuses to act on it. I've always known how to push his buttons and make him react. It's not the first time we've come to blows over something. I doubt it would be the last.

"Then how the hell is it?" My anger fades, disappearing as my heart rate slows and logic returns. Maybe I was wrong earlier. My heart wasn't the one seeing things clearly. It's the delusional part of my body. The part acting rather than thinking. In the place of my anger is something I don't want to take the time to decipher but know so well.

Pain.

"She's the new help I told you about." His voice, louder than a whisper but nowhere near a shout, cuts through me. His words paralyze me on the spot.

Fuck. Me.

"You didn't think to mention that?" I ask, trying and failing to fully understand the ramifications of his words. Trying my damndest to understand his thought process in general. Did he think this would be a good idea? Was he trying to fucking torture me?

"I would have told you it was her, but every damn time I bring up her name, you shut me down."

"Son of a . . ." I start but get distracted by Beau rubbing his jaw, a bruise darkening the surface. "Shit, man, I'm—"

"Don't worry about it. Let's get inside and get started."

He might not let me apologize, but that doesn't keep me from feeling like shit about it. Beau and I haven't physically fought since he sold one of my favorite horses without telling me about it. That was the day we decided that to keep from killing each other, he would handle the cattle and I'd handle the boarding.

I acted like a damn hotheaded teenager, a fact that shames me deeply. I've put in a lot of work to be a better man than this. And yet within twenty minutes of being in Blake's presence, I'm back to the man she left. I refuse to allow all of my hard work to go up in flames over a pretty face and long-lost crush. I've busted my ass to build something better for myself, and I refuse to ruin that now. Not because of a damn woman who left, tearing my heart straight from my chest on her way out of town.

I need to stay as far away from Blakelynn Smith as possible. It shouldn't be too hard. Point of Retreat Ranch is huge. There's enough work here for twenty people with more to spare. Plenty for both of us to do and never see each other.

When I round the corner of the barn, I almost have myself convinced until I see her cooing at Samson, a horse Beau convinced me work with a few months ago. My stomach drops. He's the hardest bastard we board and is known for showing his teeth when you least suspect it. Most days, I feel bad for the poor guy. I don't know his story, but one thing's certain. He's had a hard life.

How the hell am I supposed to keep my distance and make sure she doesn't kill herself out here?

It's going to be harder than I thought to steer clear of her. At least until she learns the ins and outs of the ranch. I make a mental list of everything I need to show her, to prepare her for.

First on the list is Samson.

CHAPTER FOUR

#hotmess

Blake

SEEING Calvin's surprise this morning was unexpected. I knew he and Beau had partnered in the ranch when Beau's dad passed, so I anticipated running into him. His reaction to seeing me, though, had me thinking that Beau never told him I was coming. I thought after all this time, I was in a place where I was ready to see him. I was wrong. Nothing could have prepared me for when he walked through the back door this morning with that dumbstruck look on his face.

If anything, he's more attractive than I remember. All six feet three inches of well-toned, hard flesh. I almost choked on coffee when he walked in the door, and that was before I even processed who it was, but when I did and the memory of his hands on my body flooded my mind, I couldn't look away.

Chills erupted across my flesh. Thankfully, Beau pulled me out of my stupor and got me out of that room and house and away from him. For now.

I should have put a little more thought into how being around him would affect things. Especially considering how close we will work together on turning the ranch around.

Beau is rubbing his jaw when they round the corner. My eyes widen and he shakes his head. When I glance at Cal, his eyes are on the ground in front of him, refusing to meet my gaze. When he looks up, I look away until he opens his mouth. I can't decide if hearing his voice is my personal heaven or hell. Until his words register, that is. Hell. Definitely hell. I'd forgotten how patronizing he could be. All in the name of protection. One day, maybe he would learn I didn't need protecting. Didn't want it.

"You should stay away from Samson here. He's too much horse for the toughest man. Best start her with Billie or Suzy." He points to the other end of the barn.

I look to Beau and see his eyes sparkle. So, Calvin doesn't know any of what I've been doing the last ten years. Interesting. I can't decide whether I'm disappointed or relieved. A little of both, I think.

"I think Samson here will be just fine, unless you think I should visit Billie first, Beau?"

Calvin glances at Beau, sure he's won round one of our verbal sparring. It takes everything I have not to laugh and rub his smug face into a pile of manure. I know it's not fair. If he hasn't kept up with my life, then he doesn't know I work with animals as often as I can. I may not be as familiar with horses as he is, but I know my way around.

"I think Samson is in good hands," Beau says, and I turn my

back on them both so Cal won't see the grin pulling across my teeth.

"Yeah, me too." I pass an apple slice to Samson from my pocket and kiss his forehead.

"It's your hand. Don't say I didn't warn you." Calvin storms off, kicking up dust as he goes, and Beau takes a step closer, coughing into the crook of his arm to hide his laughter.

"How much does he know?" I ask. It never occurred to me to have Beau fill Calvin in on everything that happened. Not that I wanted the whole world knowing the personal details of my life, anyway.

"Nothing. Every time I tried to bring you up, he walked away."

"So he doesn't know we're working together? That I'm here to give PRR a new-age facelift?" I turn to him, my brow raised.

"Nope." His answer is swift and to the point.

"What about Brad? Did you tell him?" I ask and hold my breath. I don't know why, but the thought of Calvin knowing I was engaged burns deep in my chest. I'm not sure he would even care, but a part of me, some long-forgotten piece of my heart, aches recalling the promises we made to each other the year before I lost my mom. Promises of marriage and babies and the names we had chosen for our dogs and cats and horses.

"Nope."

"Oh, shit." I don't know what else to say. The rush of relief should concern me, but I'm busy basking in its sweet release. One day, he will learn about it all. I know I can't keep it from him forever. But the idea of starting our new friendship off fresh without more broken promises and hurt feelings between us is a welcomed one. It was years ago, back when we still held the ideals of children in love, but that doesn't mean it wouldn't hurt. This makes things more interesting. At the very least, when he's being an ass to me, I know why.

"Yeah. This is going to be funny as hell. Well worth a punch to the jaw," Beau says, injecting a little humor into the situation.

I grab his face in my hand and twist it from side to side. In the low-lit barn, it's hard to see anything. "So he hit you? I thought I saw a bruise coming up but didn't think he would do that."

He grins and I shake my head. "It was just a small misunderstanding."

I wait for him to explain more, but he doesn't, so I let it go and move on. Exploring the barn, I find a lead line in a room I can only assume is the tack room. It's filled floor to ceiling with equipment for everything from riding to shoeing. In a small refrigerator, I find various vials of medicine and syringes. It's a beautiful setup, pristine and well organized. I feel like I need a library card equivalent to check something out.

"How long should we wait before we tell him Samson is mine?" I ask, returning to the main part of the barn.

The barn is wide and dirt packed with stalls on each side of the rectangular area. Above the stalls is a flat easel structure running the length of the entire barn. On the left, square hay bales are stacked to the roof. On the right, the roof slants down, creating an awning for the outdoor pasture that each stall leads out to. Calvin has placed all the mares and geldings on the right side of the barn, far away from the studs, Samson included, who is at the far end of the barn in a large stall. He's separated from the rest of the horses by an additional empty room containing feed. If I had to guess, I would say his stall was meant for a mare and her foal. Beau crosses the aisle and leans against a stall door on the left side of the barn, well out of the reach of Samson's hooves.

"Let's wait for now. He already made the biggest mistake in underestimating you."

I smile, the first real one in a while, and unlatch the door to Samson's stall.

"Let's get some fresh air, boy." I lead him out into the corral. My smile shifts into a full-fledged giggle when Calvin's eyes widen. He takes a step out of Samson's way. All these men, terrified of a misunderstood pony. He really is the biggest baby in the world, but as a rescue, he has a few quirks. One of which is his outright hatred of men.

I assume his original owner had been a male, and for whatever reason, Samson had a true distrust of all men now. When he arrived at the shelter, he had everyone scared. A few comments had been tossed around about putting him down, but when I saw him, I knew that couldn't happen. He's easily the most beautiful horse I have ever seen. His coat, a glorious shade of black, covers every inch of his body. I'd never seen a solid black horse before. Most have white stockings or a white blaze down their face. He's at least sixteen hands tall and pure muscle. I stepped to his stall much the same way I did today, and instead of pinning his ears back and charging forward, he nudged my hand with this nose, searching for the apple he smelled there.

I passed him a slice then, too, and watched as every man shook his head, confused. We formed a bond those first few weeks, but I decided the first day that I would adopt him. He deserved someone to love him. It was months before I tracked down his previous owner and his papers. I was the least surprised to learn that he came from impeccable bloodlines. I could see it in the way he carried himself. Proud and noble. It also explained a little more about his temperament. No doubt, he'd been used to breed and nothing more. Abused to cooperate. Little did they know that they couldn't break his spirit. They ignited a fire in him and a will to survive.

In the end, they couldn't handle him anymore and sold him off to another man who eventually turned him over to us.

I release his halter and sit back to watch him prance through the enclosure. His tail is held high, his neck arched he dances across the pasture. It's the only way I know to describe the graceful movement of his hooves.

I've been working on his acceptance of men for several months now. The first time Beau traveled to Arizona to see him, we spent days going through drills with Samson, but after a couple of visits, I decided to send him down here so he could get the help he really needed. I'm so thankful for Beau's help in getting him here, and maybe one day, Samson will be too. I just hope Calvin isn't too angry when he learns of my deception, but I wasn't sure he would be willing to work with Samson knowing he belongs to me.

Calvin leans against the hitch post, watching Samson trot. His jeans hug every inch of his muscled thighs, stretching across his firm ass in a way that would make a nun's mouth water. His arms are crossed at his chest, and the ball cap he's wearing blocks his eyes from my view. I want to know what he's thinking, but I don't have the guts to ask. We're walking a fine line here, and I've got a feeling things will get a lot harder before they get any easier.

Taking a deep breath, I leave Samson to his prancing and make my way over to Calvin. Time to bite the bullet. For the hundredth time during the last twelve hours, I ask myself what the hell I'm doing back here, wondering if I've made the biggest mistake yet by returning. Jumping on the hitch post next to Cal, I shake off thoughts of failure and mistakes. Maybe I screwed up. Maybe I didn't. I can't worry about it right now while my palms are sweating and my heart palpitating. The shock of first seeing Cal has worn off a little, but the idea of working and talking to him without Beau around to whisk me off if I need him is terrifying. Luckily, I've spent the last few years overcoming my fears, and Calvin Hunt has nothing on stage fright.

"So, where should we start?" I ask hesitantly.

"Hmph," he grunts, stepping away and leaving me to follow after him.

Grouchy ass.

I match his stride step for step once I catch up to him. "Where are we headed?" I try again to make small talk. This isn't easy for me, either, coming back home, admitting defeat, and then having to practically grovel . . . okay, I'm not groveling. I'm a successful, attractive woman. I don't need or want any man at the moment, especially not Calvin Hunt, but I would like to be on speaking terms with him.

When he lifts his left foot, I lift mine. After a few minutes, he catches on and swaps up his gait to mix me up, but I'm a pro at this. He should remember that. He spins on the ball of his foot and changes direction. I spin with him, and then when he stops, I stop. This time, I copy the movement of his hands too, swinging mine loosely at my sides. Before I know it, we're back at the barn. Calvin sits on the swing hanging from a large pecan tree in front, and I huff out an exasperated sigh. "That's cheating," I say with a frown. It's a fake frown. I push my bottom lip out as far as I can, wondering if he will follow through. Years ago, as children, we would play this game together, and it always ended the same way, with Cal quitting and me winning.

"No, that's called winning." I smile when he says his line.

"Cheater, cheater, pumpkin eater—" I call out, but he cuts me off.

"Loser, loser, double loser."

It's the first time I've heard his laugh in eleven years, and the deep, rumbling sound does things to me I'm not expecting. My answering smile isn't forced, and it isn't fake, put on for an audience. This feels good. Right.

Almost as soon as I think the thought, Cal sobers. His laughter dies, and the smile that was moments ago gracing his face vanishes into thin air.

"I need to make a call." With that, he stands and stomps in the direction of Beau's. The swing is still dancing in the wind from his hasty departure. I calm it and then I sit in the still warm spot he just vacated.

CHAPTER FIVE

#whyme

Calvin

TODAY HAS BEEN complete and total hell. Sharp lightning-quick pain shoots down my hand every time I close my fist. Not that I don't deserve it for hitting Beau. Hell, I deserve a more than a few aches for that stupid act. No amount of physical pain in the world could compare to being forced to work beside Blake all day. Every time she speaks to me, I bounce between being overjoyed that she is home and wanting to stick a knife in my ear and cut out the sweet sound of her voice. It doesn't help that she keeps reminding me of the when she was mine and I was hers and we were fucking happy.

She's literally making me lose my mind, and she's only been here a day.

I slide onto the bar stool and tap the bar. Little Janie

McElroy pulls a Bud from the ice cooler and pops the top before placing it in front of me. It's still a shock every time I see her working the bar. I can't believe she's old enough to drive, much less drink and work at a bar. Too many years have passed without my knowledge. Memories lost to time.

"Give me two fingers of that Jack, too, while you're here." I point to the Jack on the back-wall display.

"Bad day?" She sets the glass down. I pick it right back up, turning it down in one pass, and hand the glass back. She refills it and sets it back in front of me.

"You could say that."

If you had asked me a week ago—hell, ten hours ago—if I'd be able to handle seeing Blake again, I would have shrugged it off and not given it another thought. I didn't need to. Blake left and she wasn't coming back. Or at least, I didn't think she was. Then she turned up, sending my life into a tailspin of questions and emotions I didn't want to deal with. Not only was she back, but it looked like she planned to stay for a while.

I'm not sure I can handle it.

Blakelynn isn't the same girl who ran out of this town at the stroke of midnight on her eighteenth birthday. She's grown, and I don't mean physically. Although I guess that's true too. I spent the whole day wanting to avoid her and not being able to take my eyes off her. Every once in a while, time would disappear and it would be like it used to be, and then I'd remember the pain and the longing and the loss. The problem was that I remembered it less and less the longer I spent with her.

Her hair is longer and maybe a little lighter than I remember, but I imagine it's just as soft as the last time I ran my fingers through it. Some things haven't changed at all. Like her warm honey brown eyes, even if the innocence in them is long gone, and the single dimple that appeared when she tried to hide her smile. Speaking of, her smile shines just as brightly, lighting up the room, but those carefree smiles come less often and not at all for me. Not that I'm trying to make her smile, but damn, I would kill for one to be directed at me instead of at the animals.

"Grab me a Bud too, Janie?" Beau calls out, sliding onto the bar stool next to me. I lift my beer and take a long draw.

Janie passes him a beer and glances between us, her gaze hoovering on Beau a little longer than normal. She looks like she wants to say something but thinks better of it. Good idea, Janie.

"Today was good," Beau says, taking a pull from his bottle.

I bark out a laugh. If he thinks today was good, I'd hate to see a bad day.

"Well, it could have been worse," he tries again.

I turn to face him then. "Could it? How the hell could it have been worse? You hired my ex—hell, not just my ex but the girl who destroyed me—to revamp the entire ranch. I'm still not sure what the hell that means. Maybe I'm blind, but I thought we were doing pretty fucking well, but maybe that's something else you've been keeping from me."

Janie walks to the other end of the bar to give us as much privacy as she can, but I see her eyes widen in realization when I mention my ex. It's no secret that I was head over heels in love with Blakelynn. I had been young, but even then, I knew I wanted her for the rest of my life. She was it for me. I've tried dating a few women since she left, but I cut them loose almost as soon as I start. It's not fair to them or me to drag out something when I know I'm not one hundred percent committed to it.

TINLEY BLAKE

How the fuck I'm supposed to commit to another woman when I still compare each one of them to the girl who got away, I'll never know. It's been easier to stay single and put all of my free time into building up the ranch, making a life I can be proud of even if I don't have anyone to share it with. Now Beau is telling me that all that work still isn't enough, and his bright idea is to bring the woman I can't get out of my system back into town to make it better.

I have no doubt that she will. Blake has always been great at shit like that. But what about when she leaves again? I don't believe in fate or karma or everything working out for the best. I don't have a fucking fairy godmother who can wave a magical wand and make all my dreams come true. Blake will leave again. This isn't her home anymore. She outgrew us years ago.

Who is going to pick up the pieces when she packs up and heads back to her big city? Who's going to make sure everything doesn't fall apart again?

"We're doing fine, but that doesn't mean we can't do better. Blake's got some great ideas that I think you would like if you'd just hear her out."

I laugh at that too. Does he think I don't want to listen to her? I'd love to do nothing but listen to the words—any words— fall from her perfect rosy lips. But it's more than that. Her words come with a price. And change. I've worked my ass off helping to rebuild the ranch into something Beau and I could both be proud of after his dad ran it into the ground. It's taken a lot of time and determination. And now, she's going to waltz in and start calling the shots, changing everything up when we've just got it running smoothly again.

"You should have run it by me."

"I did. I brought it up at least a dozen times, and you didn't want to hear it. The ranch is earning a profit for the first time in years, and I know a lot of that is because of you. But the competition doesn't care how long we spent climbing out of debt. They didn't wait for us to get on our feet, and now they are working with state-of-the-art equipment and have marketing budgets the size of our yearly spending account. We need a fresh start. A makeover. And that just happens to be what Blake does."

"Do you really think she can pull it off?" I already know the answer, but I want to hear him say it.

"Hell, yeah. I know she can."

"And I have to work with her?" I know the answer to this too. A part of me is grateful. If another man had been working with her day in and day out, I would be less focused than I am now. Every thought would be centered on her and what the two of them were doing. I'm not normally a jealous man, but Blake brings out the very best and the absolute worst in me.

"This part of it is yours. I handle the cattle and you handle the horses. Right?"

"Fuck me," I say, exasperated.

"Just do me a favor and take it easy on her. It wasn't easy for her to come back here."

I nod and toss back the Jack. That makes two of us. I didn't think I would ever see her again—wasn't prepared to. Now I have to work with her every day on some bullshit plan I didn't even agree to.

Revamp the ranch? What does that entail? I'm not stupid. I know the profit we're earning is barely enough to keep the bank account positive. It's been a hard ass road, trying to climb out of debt and run a business we could both be proud of. An honest business.

I'm sure Blake is the best of the West and can pull bunnies out of hats and shit, but that doesn't mean I want to be stuck working side by side with her every day. She didn't even pretend to be bothered by it, which pisses me off even more. I waited and watched for any signs of discomfort today. Not sure how I would handle it, but the fact that she was able to treat me just like any other Billy Bob off the street fucking bothered me.

Tomorrow, I plan to show her how it feels. Lifting my beer, I chug the rest of it down and tap the bar for another. I swear her scent still clings to me, burning the thought of her into my mind.

Fuck. Me.

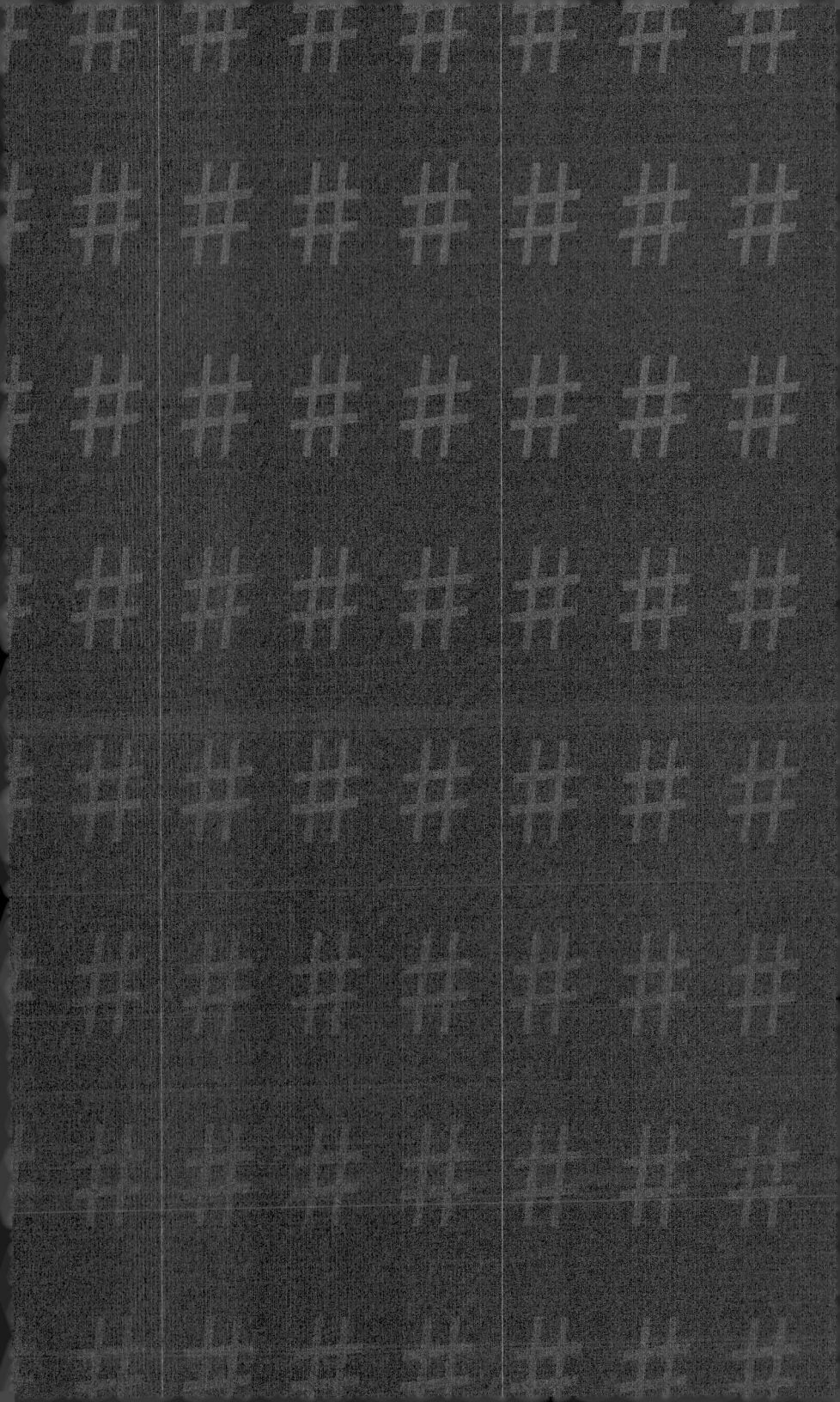

CHAPTER SIX

#tiredofhisshit

Blake

I'M NOT sure what I expected to happen over the weekend. Maybe a relaxing, calm couple of days before the fun began on Monday, but Calvin had other ideas. He showed up Saturday morning at the crack of dawn with a list of things he wanted to go over with me. *To keep me safe.* I would have laughed at the idea if I wasn't so damn tired. I'm not sure what caused the change in him, but from Friday afternoon to Saturday morning, he had become someone else.

All day Friday, he sulked like my appearance in town was a personal attack on him. Every once in a while, the armor he'd strapped on slipped and he would joke or laugh, but not long and not often. When he showed up Saturday, all that was gone. He was all business.

I kinda missed the sullen looks. At least I understood those.

My phone rings, and I run across the room to grab it before it goes to voicemail. The first of the investors is arriving this morning and I still don't have a shirt on. I lay in the bed all night, tossing and turning when I finally fell asleep. This shit with Calvin has my mind twisted, out of the game. I need to focus if I'm going to get the help we need to turn this place around.

Breathless and stressed to the max, I answer the phone. "Hello?"

"Hello, Miss Smith. The GPS says I am five minutes away."

"Okay, excellent. I'll meet you outside."

Searching through the suitcase I haven't had time to unpack yet, I find a semi-clean shirt and toss it over my head before running down the stairs. I've barely slipped into my boots when I hear the gravel crunch signaling the arrival of my first potential investor.

I lined up several before I left Arizona. Not many people were interested in hearing about farms or ranches, but an investor didn't care what the product was as long as it would make them money. And I truly believe Point of Retreat could make money, but first it needs an overhaul.

I open the door expecting to see the face of Mr. Davenport, but instead, I find Calvin. Neo is racing into the pasture like he has every morning since I've been here, only returning once he's winded and thirsty. "What are you doing here?" I ask, forgetting to be docile.

"I work here. Or did you forget that already?"

"No. I just. Shit." I stammer the words out.

"What is it?"

"I've got investors coming right this second, actually, to view the property, and I just can't deal with you on top of it."

"Deal with me?"

"Calvin, cut the shit. You've been distant and petty as hell all weekend, and that's fine if you want to be mean to me, if you need to pay me back for hurting you or whatever. I can handle it, but right now, I need to be focused on these people showing up so I can help the ranch, and I can't do that and tiptoe around you too."

I can tell I've offended him or pissed him off. I'm not sure which, and I don't have time to figure it out because Mr. Davenport pulls in at that moment.

"Shit. Please just don't be a dick to them, okay? They are here to help."

I leave him and greet my first potential investor, plastering a smile the size of Texas on my face. I take Mr. Davenport around, pointing out things I'd like to change and sharing my ideas with him. He seems interested, but then again, they usually do. When we're done, he tells me he will be in contact. I wave goodbye and then rush inside to grab a quick cup of coffee before the next investor arrives.

Cal is at the table when I walk in. He passes me a mug filled with cream just the way I like it. I take the offered mug the way a bomb tech would an explosive, with the utmost care and a little concern.

"Thanks?" I don't mean for the statement to curl into a question, but it does.

"I've been an ass. I'm sorry. Is there anything I can help with?"

"Do you mean that?"

"Fuck, Blake. Of course, I mean it. I've been busting my ass to help this place, and if you know a way I can do that, then I'm all yours."

My pulse jumps when he says *I'm all yours*. Even if I know he doesn't mean it that way, it's still an echo of a promise he made to me years ago.

"I could use you. You know this place better than me. You have the passion they need to see. Tossing money at something is one thing, but if they know the people working here have a true desire to make it work, then it could push them to say yes."

"I can do that."

"I hope you're sure because our next visitor just pulled in."

As soon as the mother—daughter duo step out of their Range Rover, Cal turns on the Southern charm. I'd laugh if it wasn't working so well. We walk the property while Calvin explains to them the purpose of everything we come across. I try to interject and lead the tour back to task, but my words fall on deaf ears. I'm not sure which one of the two is flirting more, but if Cal notices, he doesn't show it. By the time we make it back to their vehicle, the mother has lost two layers of clothing and the daughter is pretending to limp so she can lean on Cal's *big, strong arm*.

As they drive away, I lean over holding my stomach and laugh so hard I really might pee my pants. "Oh, Cal, my foot! Can you carry me?"

"Shut up."

"Aw, don't be such a sourpuss."

"Who's being a sourpuss?" Beau asks, appearing out of nowhere. I jump and squeal before laughing some more., this time at myself.

"Calvin made a few lady friends," I say, trying to catch Beau up between fits of laughter.

"Not friends. They're potential investors, and I was being nice," Cal says, blushing.

"You should have seen them. They were falling all over him, worshiping him like a prized pig."

"You're just mad they ignored you the whole time," Cal says, taking a dig at me.

"Do you think they will invest?" Beau asks, and Cal shrugs.

"I think they might, if for no other reason than to see Cal again." His hand reaches out lightning-fast, but I sidestep and dance out of his grasp, giggling like a schoolgirl.

The rest of the afternoon follows the same pattern. Investors arrive, we escort them around the property, Cal fills in areas I don't know yet, and then we pick at each other until the next arrives. It's nice, this change in him. He reminds me of the old Cal, the one I couldn't help but fall in love with. The Cal I'd planned to spend my forever with.

CHAPTER SEVEN

#spilledcoffee

Blake

THE MORNING IS cool and crisp. A welcomed reprieve after the blistering ninety degrees yesterday. Dew glistens on each blade of grass, a welcome reminder that fall is coming and with it change, but not yet. One thing I remember clearly about Alabama is the false fall. Every year, a month or so before actual fall, we would have a week of cool temps. The leaves would take their final breath before curling and the grass would slow its growth. Couples would line their porches with mustard yellow mums and break out the fall décor, only for the temps to rise again the next week.

I spent most of the day walking and exploring the ranch yesterday. It would make promoting it a lot easier if I knew it inside and out. Not much has changed in the eleven years since

I was last here. I don't know what I expected, but in a lot of ways, I felt like I had stepped back in time.

The only thing that has changed is me.

I don't know how I fit here anymore. If I fit at all.

"Morning." Calvin appears out of nowhere, startling me. I jump, sloshing coffee over the rim of the mug.

"Hey. You scared me." I wipe my hand down the side of my jeans and set the mug on the porch rail.

Calvin Hunt has changed too. Gone is the boy I grew up chasing through corn fields and cotton patches. In his place is a man, rugged and masculine. He gives off an aura of strength, and coupled with his nonchalant attitude, it's enough to leave any girl guessing.

"Sleep well?" *Really, Blake?* Why the hell am I asking him how he slept? Judging by the look on his face, he seems to be wondering the same thing. Raising his brow in question, he steps on the porch next to me and I forget to breathe. If I thought I couldn't concentrate when he was in the yard, that is nothing compared to now when he is inches away from me, leaning against the porch railing without a care in the world.

He's wearing another pair of those damn jeans again, the ones that hug his legs snugly. Not so tight that he can't bend over or squat, but fitted enough that his ass is on display. His shirt, light blue and untucked, makes the colored freckles in his eyes pop. His arms are lean but muscular. *Strong*, I think, recalling the bruise on Beau's jaw. Capable of hurting someone, but if I remember correctly, they also feel like heaven wrapped around me.

A lustful sigh escapes when I recall what else his body is capable of doing. The way he moves on top of me, hard and sure, soft and vulnerable. I shouldn't be thinking about him like this. Hell, I shouldn't be thinking about anything like this. I left Mesa and the drama of men behind. It was time for a fresh start. A new beginning. Dammit, there's work to be done.

I don't have time for butterflies or daydreaming.

Calvin pulls a red handkerchief from his back pocket and pushes it with the gentlest touch to my chest. The breath I was inhaling stops, trapped in my lungs. "You've got coffee there," he says. I stare into his eyes, my hand on his hand on my chest, unable to look away, unable to move. Held paralyzed by his touch. Shocking electric waves course along my skin, straight to my core where they pool, warming me until I think I may combust.

"I think I got it." He doesn't move his hand. I register his words in the distant part of my brain that is still functioning. The rest has short-circuited with one touch from him. Not even a romantic touch, just the long-missed feel of his skin against my own.

"Th–thank you." He's turned me into a stuttering mess. When he pulls his hand away, some brain function returns. Not much, just enough to exhale the breath I've been holding captive. My body betrays me, selfish bitch that it is. Calvin is still inches from my side. I can feel the heat coming off him, and it makes my skin break out in chills, which makes no freaking sense, considering the sun has officially broken across the horizon and with it, the raging heat of Alabama's summertime.

This close, I take in all of his features. He needs a haircut. The russet brown strands that perfectly match his tobacco colored eyes are starting to curl around his ears. My fingers twitch, begging to run through it. His full lips are parted, his own breath pushing between them in a warm caress. He leans toward me, and I pull my eyes from his mouth only for them to jump right back there in anticipation. His shoulder brushes against my chest. I swear he can feel my heart beating inside my chest, he's that close, but instead of kissing me like I expect, he grabs my coffee cup and then, turning on his heel, walks into the house. I slump into the white rocker and for the next five minutes question my sanity.

What the hell am I thinking? Of course, Calvin Hunt isn't trying to kiss me. I left town, leaving him behind with nothing but his memories and an aching heart. I bury my face in my hands and take a few deep, calming breaths. "Get it together, Blake."

The slam of the screen door makes me jump for the second time in the last ten minutes, and this time, Calvin barks out a laugh. "Why so jumpy, Sugar?"

I narrow my eyes at his use of the stereotypical endearment and stand, taking a step toward him. If he wants to play this game, I can play it better. "Long night." I wink. "Not a lot of rest." I leave him to interpret that however he sees fit. His eyes narrow, his mouth hardening, and I give myself an imaginary fist bump.

Calvin- 0

Blake- 1

Yes, I know it's petty to lead him to believe I was up doing sexy, inappropriate things, but I can't help it. He already got the better of me twice and left me leaning in for a kiss he had no plan of offering. In a move of pure luck, Beau walks out and saves me from embarrassing myself further.

"Ready, Buttercup?" Beau asks, pulling my ponytail.

"Yep," I say, taking a step off the porch.

I'm about three steps ahead of the guys when I hear Calvin ask Beau, "Sleep well last night?"

I spin around and take a few steps backward. Beau is eyeballing Cal like he's grown three heads and eaten half of his cattle. "Not really. Late night," he says.

"Hmph," Cal replies. I spin back around and try to contain the grin stretching across my face.

"Alone?" Calvin asks. I can't contain the laugh that slips out. Beau doesn't have a chance to reply before Calvin detours and heads to the feed room.

"Wanna explain what that was all about?" Beau asks, catching up to me.

"Hmm?" I feign innocence.

"Blake . . ."

Ugh. Why do all the men in my life want so much from me? Can't a girl have a secret? Sheesh.

"He asked why I was so jumpy, and I didn't want to tell him it was because I didn't know how to act around him, so I told him I had a late night and didn't get much sleep. If you know what I mean."

"And then I . . ." His eyes widen at the implication. "Shit, Blake, are you trying to get me killed here?"

"No." Laughter bubbles up from somewhere deep inside now, and I can't stop it. "I'll set him straight if he gets too upset. Don't worry." I pinch his arm. "Now, how was your night? Was that Janie I saw darting out of here before the sun came up this morning?"

Beau's hand clamps over my mouth. "Shh. You saw that?" I nod and lick his hand. He pulls it back, wiping it on his jeans. "It's nothing, really."

"Mmmhmm, sure it isn't," I say, mock kissing the air.

"God, you're such a damn baby," he says. I slap him hard, and he laughs, catching my hand in his when I swing again. Cal

59

walks back in at that moment, and I die on the spot, laughing so hard I'm bending at the waist.

"Beau. Can I see you for a sec?" Cal ignores my presence, looking only at Beau. He's in a worse mood now than earlier. The tension in the barn reaches all new heights. Beau turns to follow Cal outside, holding his hands together at his chest. "Pray for me," he mouths before stepping out of the barn.

I really shouldn't be messing with Calvin like this, and for a second, I'm worried he might think something serious is going on with me and Beau. I decide to clear it up before Cal gets his pants in a wad, but when I walk out of the barn, they're both gone.

After a lengthy search of the front, I pause, listening. All I hear is the sound of the ranch waking. They've both disappeared. Shrugging my shoulders, I head back into the barn. I've got a crap ton of work I need to do if I plan on having the new website for Point of Retreat Ranch live by the end of the week. I had hoped I would get more time with Calvin while learning, but it appears he is hell-bent on avoiding me at all costs. It's for the best.

After the way my body reacted to him this morning, I wasn't sure I would be able to control my actions. If he'd leaned in and captured my mouth with his, I wouldn't—couldn't—have stopped him. What's worse is I knew I wouldn't even want to. I wasn't expecting all these urges to come back when I saw him. For some reason, I figured I'd be able to treat him the same way I treated Beau, like a really good friend. We had a past, but that didn't mean we couldn't have a future as something else, right?

If the ache between my thighs were any indicator, I was more than just wrong.

I was slap fucking crazy.

Last night had been a long night for me, and not only because I was working. I tossed and turned in the bed for hours trying to find a comfortable position, finally falling asleep sometime in the early morning hours only to wake again, pulse racing, legs clenched tight, with Cal's name on my lips and his body my only desire.

I've been trying to erase all thought of him since.

I said trying. I'm not perfect, okay?

There are two things I value above all else in life.

My sleep and my coffee.

Calvin Hunt is screwing with them both. The first by being so damn sexy I couldn't get him out of my head and fall asleep, and the second by scaring me half to death and making me spill my coffee. He deserved payback, but that would require my thinking about him, and I'm not doing that anymore.

I'm not.

If I said it enough, maybe it would come true. Isn't that some kind of law? No, wait. That's not right.

If it can go wrong, it will.

Still pretty damn accurate.

"Argh. Men!" I stomp my foot and recommit to ignoring them all. Samson paws his stall wall, calling for my attention, and I smile.

Maybe not all men. Just the two-legged variety.

CHAPTER EIGHT

#notagain

Calvin

I'LL KILL HIM.

I swear, I will.

Blake is off limits. He knows that. I shouldn't even have to say the words. What kind of man goes after the girl who tore out your best friend's heart? A shitty one.

"Calm down, Cal. I know what you're thinking." Beau says, stepping outside.

"Do you?" I ask, climbing into the horse trailer. I've got to get this thing cleaned out and ready to transport Billie back to her place this weekend.

"Yeah, pretty sure I do. Blake's just fucking with you. She said you started it," Beau says, leaning against the trailer door.

"Did she now?" I think back to our interaction earlier,

wondering. Is it possible she wanted me to kiss her as much as I wanted to?

I had been about to. God help me, but I couldn't be around the woman and not fucking want her. She was perfection. All five feet eight inches of her. I grin, imagining the torturous things I'd like to do with her sly mouth.

Vixen.

Beau shakes his head back and forth. "What the hell did I think would happen, bringing you two together?"

"What?" I ask, feigning innocence.

"Really? Both of you are going to cause me to go to an early grave. I can't deal with y'all. I'm going to check the cattle. Help her with whatever she needs, and for God's sake, keep your hands to yourself." He says the last as sternly as he can without sounding like a fool. Beau the playboy himself. He couldn't fault my train of thought, no matter how much he wanted to.

"No promises," I call back to him with a sly smile.

He's mumbling to himself as he stomps off. I wipe the grin off my face before going to find Blake. This could be fun. As long as she's willing. There aren't any rules against having fun as long as neither of us gets our feelings involved. Right?

If she wants a replay of earlier times, I'm all for it. This time, I won't make the same mistakes. No feelings, no pain.

I find her bent over, taking a photo of Samson's hooves from under the stall door. My first instinct is to yell at her to get the hell away from him, but that would give away my presence. I sneak up behind her, getting as close as I can. "What are you doing?" She bolts upright, startled, just like I'd hoped. I hadn't realized how close I was standing until the round cheeks of her ass graze my crotch.

It's been too damn long since I had a woman if all it takes is a brushing of flesh for it to come alive. I take a step back and turn to adjust myself.

"What the hell, Calvin? Do you just enjoy scaring the shit out of me?" Blake screams at me, her voice full of injustice. I love seeing her frazzled.

I wrap my fingers around her shoulder and spin her around so I can check her pants. My hands refuse to release her once I have her in my grasp.

"What the hell are you doing?" she asks, her own hands slapping at me until I let her go.

"I don't see any shit stains, but I can wait here if you need to go change."

She slaps my arm. Hard. "Har-har. You think you're funny, don't you?"

"Nah, Sugar, you're the funny one." I take a step closer, invading her personal space. Her breath hitches and her arms drop to her side. I lean in, passing her lips with nothing more than a wisp of air between ours, and whisper in her ear. "Beau? Really?" I ask and then turn on my heel and walk away, leaving her a sputtering mess.

"Ahh!" she yells, stomping after me. "I'm going to kick your ass for that, Calvin Hunt."

I stop and spin around so fast she runs straight into my chest. "Would you like me to strip? I can give you better access," I offer. The sweetest rosy tint creeps up her neck and spreads across her cheeks. Grinning, I reach for my belt buckle.

"Screw you," she says, pushing away from me.

Letting go of my belt, I reach out and grab her arm. My hand slides down to her wrist, then her hand that I take in my own. "What do you think I'm offering, Sugar?" It takes great strength to keep a straight face.

65

"Ahh. Shut up and stop twisting my words." She stomps her foot on the ground, and dust billows up around us. I laugh because it's such a Blake thing to do. She's never been able to handle someone getting the best of her.

"Would you rather I twist you around?" I ask and spin her around. When I pull her flush against my hardened body, she gasps. "You always did like it best like this," I whisper in her ear, causing her to shiver.

Chills erupt along her arms, across her chest, and up her neck. I run my tongue along her ear before letting her go. "Calvin!" She tries to sound indignant, but it sounds more like a breathy moan than an angry protest.

"Wow, Sugar, already screaming my name and I haven't even touched you yet." I haven't had this much fun in a long time. Seeing her flustered lightens my spirits. I don't know what that says about my character. Nothing good, I'm sure. But it is what it is. I take two steps out the door, leaving her in the middle of the barn alleyway. This time, when I walk away, she doesn't follow me.

"I hate you," she yells and then stomps her foot again. "Argh!"

Sure you do, Blake. You hate that you want me. I understand. A part of me hates that I want you too. I don't understand how any part of my body could still crave the woman who destroyed me, but the bulge in my pants is a clear indicator that some parts of my body don't hold grudges.

Ten minutes later, I'm starting to wonder if I pushed too hard or came on too strongly with Blake. She hasn't reappeared. Maybe I should take her absence as confirmation that she isn't interested in playing around, but then she walks back into the barn yard and all thought scatters in the wind.

Gone are the boot-cut jeans and worn-out T-shirt. In their place are shorts so tiny that if she were to bend over, I swear I'd be able to see her panties. *If she has any on.* Shit. Now I'm thinking about her lack of panties, and the boner I thought I had under control is making its reappearance.

She's wearing a white crop top that shows off every sweet morsel of skin between the waist of her shorts and the hem of her shirt. I want to run my tongue along that skin over and over again. She's let her hair down, and it falls in dusty blonde waves across her shoulders. The only thing she hasn't changed is her boots, and to be honest, I kind of wish she had.

"Nice boots." The words squeak out. I can't think of anything else to say. I'm surprised I was able to form a thought at all.

"Photo shoot time," she says, tossing me a camera I hadn't even noticed she was carrying. I twist it around and try to figure out what is where and what the hell she wants me to do with it.

"Photo shoot?" I ask.

"Yep, and you're the cameraman. But don't worry, I've done this a hundred times so I'll walk you through it," she says, laying a blanket down across a few hay bales. When she climbs on them, she faces me on her stomach, her legs crossed behind her, her face propped in her hands. The picture of innocence. But I know better. I can see the gleam in her eye, daring me to give up. To call a truce.

Eleven years ago, I might have let her win.

"How do I work this thing?" I ask her.

"Aim it. You can see the picture on the back of the camera, and then press the fat button on the top."

I line the camera up with her and press the button. The shutter whines and then clicks, taking the picture. I take a few more of her lying there facing me. I kind of enjoy this. If offers a new angle, a new perspective of Blakelynn Smith.

She's always been a confident woman. I don't think a day went by that she didn't know what she wanted or have a plan to get it. I used to think I was part of that plan, but then she left and I was still here, picking up the pieces.

Blake sits up on her knees, her legs tucked behind her. She grabs a handful of hay and tosses it in the air. Her shirt rides up, showing off a jeweled belly button ring. Tilting her head back, she laughs, watching the hay fall. I've never seen someone so fucking beautiful. She literally takes my breath away and fills my lungs with life. It's simultaneous. It's perfection.

We go through several positions, each one sexier than the last. I've never taken so many pictures in my life, and yet I could take a hundred thousand more if it was of her and still not have enough.

"Your turn."

"My what?" I ask, sure I've misheard her.

"Oh, come one. Just sit there and relax. It'll be fun."

"Fun?" I swear I can string together more words, just not right this second. She grabs the camera and gives me a shove toward the hay bales. I don't have the slightest clue of what to do.

"Just relax. Pretend you're taking a break or thinking about something important."

I stare straight ahead, my eyes locked on hers behind the camera. She's got to be kidding me. I can't think of anything important right now. My every thought is on her. And all the ways I want to peel her out of those shorts.

"Seriously?"

"What?" I ask.

She sets the camera down and grabs my shoulders, rubbing her hands up and down them. "Relax. You're so tense. Try to loosen up." She shakes me back and forth and I let her.

"Good. Now open your legs up a little," she says, pushing my legs apart with her own. "Now lean forward. Try resting your elbows on your thighs." I follow her lead and wait while she takes a few pictures.

"Okay," she says, pushing my shoulder back. "Now lie back and put one arm over your face like you're shielding the sun." I toss my arm over my eyes like I would if I were hiding from the light, and she huffs out a sigh of annoyance.

"Not like that. I want to still see your eyes."

"Well, then, I'm not shielding from the sun, then, am I?"

"Pull your arm up," she says, leaning across my lap, her body pressed to mine. When she moves my arm, I open my eyes to find her staring at my mouth. This time, I don't think twice about it. I lean forward and capture her mouth with my own, wrapping my arms around her. Her lips part, her breath rushing out. I slide my hands under her short shirt along her back. She spreads her legs, straddling my lap. When she feels my erection, she moans into my mouth and I almost lose what's left of my sanity right then. I pull her in tight, lifting my hips to grind against the warmth between her legs. My leg bumps against something hard, and I push it to the side until it falls to the ground with a shallow thump.

"Shit, the camera," she says, sliding off my lap and trying to twist around. I slide my palms up her thighs and squeeze her ass hard. Fuck the camera.

CHAPTER NINE

#hayinmyass

Blake

"THERE ARE other things far more interesting than that damn camera. Let me show you," he says, running his fingers under the edge of my shorts. The smirk that heats my core spreads across his face. He's always been able to light me on fire with nothing more than a look. A fact he seems to have remembered. His finger slides under my panties and the sparks ignite.

"Shit." My body leans into his hand. I abandon all thoughts of the camera. For a fleeting second, I question whether this is a good idea. I've only been back here for a few weeks. Things between Cal and me were just now settling into a norm that I was happy with. *Would sleeping with him ruin that? Am I willing to risk it?*

His finger curls into me. The callused tip rubs against the slickened flesh between my thighs. My legs shake, almost giving out. My head falls back, my eyes closed. I've never wanted to be consumed as much as I do at this moment.

And then all thought vanishes, leaving nothing but desire in its wake. He pulls me onto his lap so I'm straddling his hips once again. I lean forward, taking his mouth with my own. His rock-hard cock juts against my belly through our clothes. Not close enough. *I need more.*

"See?" he says, grabbing my ass and aligning my core with his bulging cock. Wetness pools between my legs, and our mouths collide, tongues searching, demanding, claiming each other. Calvin gathers my hair behind my neck to twist it around his wrist and then pulls my head back, exposing my neck. His lips and then tongue kiss a path down my throat. His teeth graze my flesh, and I shiver, my nipples hardening. Panting, I close my eyes again and move my hands under the hem of his shirt, sliding them up his hard abs and exploring his smooth chest.

When he pulls back, releasing my hair, I open my eyes to protest. There is no need, though. He's only making space between us to gather his shirt and pull it over his head. He wastes no time in doing the same with mine. My blood pounds in my ears as he removes my bra. I hope like hell he's not speaking to me right now because his words would be falling on deaf ears. That flash of awareness that we're in the barn where anyone could enter at any time flashes through my thoughts but dissipates just as fast as it developed.

Pressing my warm, naked breasts against his bare chest, a sigh escapes me. He groans, thrusting up against my willing core while flicking his tongue over the edge of my nipples, first one and then the other.

When he sucks the puckered tip into his mouth, I shudder

and arch my back, begging for more. I can feel him gazing at me and hold my breath until he circles my waist with his powerful hands, pulling me down flush with him. He nuzzles my cheek with his nose, and I feel him smiling.

"What?" I whisper.

"You hate me." He tosses out my earlier retort still wearing that damn smirk that he doubles with a wink. It's confirmed. I've melted on the spot.

"Oh, well, what had happened was . . ." I reply with a teasing grin, lifting myself back up. I scratch the tips of my nails down his chest over the sharp ridges of his abs to the top of his jeans.

"Stand up," he orders, nudging his hips against mine, and it's all I can do to remove myself from the heat of his body. Standing over Cal with the hot sun warming my back through the barn door opening, I should feel anxious or self-conscious as he devours me with his eyes, but all I feel is desired.

Cal reaches up to unbutton my shorts. I place my hands on my hips and shake my head back and forth. He drops his hands and his face twists in confusion. Shooting him a wicked grin, I begin the process of unbuttoning and peeling them off myself, taking my sweet time. I shake my hips from side to side in an exotic dance as old as time. I leave my panties hanging off my hips and kneel to remove his jeans, never taking my eyes from his.

Dark lust floods his bright brown eyes, turning them black. His need matches my own.

The glory of Calvin Hunt naked is unmatched by any sight I have ever seen. His body at eighteen was beautiful, familiar. Now, he's a piece of art. I could sit and study the hard lines and muscular dips for hours, days, years, and still never tire of him.

My thick blonde hair blankets my body in a curtain of soft waves. I rise from my knees slowly. Never losing contact with my skin, he slips his fingers into the edge of my panties and drags them down my legs. The path his finger takes blazes.

I step out of them and closer to him.

He closes his eyes as his hands travel the length of my legs from my ankles to my ass where he stops to pull me astride him again. I hover over the tip of his steely length, every muscle in my body trembling as I grip his shoulders and sink down, impaling myself on his throbbing head. Slowly, I stretch to accommodate his size. Our eyes close for only a moment as I take him inside me. A guttural moan from deep in his throat escapes his lips.

"You're so tight. You feel so fucking good, Blake," he says through gritted teeth.

I nod my head, agreeing, unable to form the words. Gripping my hips, he glides me off him until I am suspended just over the tip of his thick cock. I inhale, ripe with anticipation, and follow his gaze to where our bodies connect. We watch together as he eases me back down, gripping my hips, his fingers digging into my flesh. I know he's grasping at the last threads of his control. I am too. I can't even remember the last time I had sex, and this, well, I haven't been touched like this in even longer. Maybe ever.

He's holding back for me, waiting, the model of patience, but that's not what I want. Taking over, I push down on him, drawing him deeper and deeper. When I reach the base, I circle my hips, grinding into him and creating the friction I need to make me soar before sliding back up his steely length again in a delicious rhythm. We grip each other tightly, skin blazing, climbing, climbing, climbing.

Calvin takes my mouth in a deep, winding kiss. I whimper in bliss and manage to string together enough words to form an intelligible sentence. "I'm going to come," I groan into his mouth.

"Wait for me."

"Can't," I shout and then fall, fall, fall over the edge. His hands circle my waist, his hips lifting, pounding into me over and over as my legs clench, tightening around him. My body pulses with the waves of my orgasm. His cock thickens even more, and his teeth nip at my bottom lip, a guttural moan escaping as he spills into me. We cling together, our bodies slick with the remnants of the act coating my thighs.

"Holy fuck."

"Yeah," I reply. There's not much else to say. I lean back across his thighs and wait for my pulse to return to normal. His cock jumps inside me, already hardening again, but this time, my own cravings aren't clogging my thoughts. I sit up and glance around, making sure we don't have any visitors, and then I stand and shimmy back into my shorts before grabbing my bra and shirt. His cum is sticky between my legs. Calvin watches me through half-closed eyes. His confident smirk is back.

"God, that was . . ." I search my vocabulary for an adjective to fit but come up empty. There are no words to adequately describe what that was. I'm more relaxed than I have been in the better part of a year. This could have been a huge mistake. An inevitable mistake. Two people with the past we share can't remain as only friends. I knew that coming here, but it doesn't change the facts. Neither of us wants this. We tried once already, and it ended in heartache and loss. Calvin may desire my body, but that's all he will ever want from the girl who crushed his heart.

Once I have my clothes somewhat arranged, I grab the camera from the ground. After checking to make sure it didn't break in the fall, I snap a few photos of Cal lying naked on the bales of hay. He reaches for the camera, but I back away, snapping more.

"What are you doing?"

"Don't worry. I won't share them with anyone."

"Fine, but I get all of yours and you can't share them either."

"Seriously? I needed those."

"Deal or Delete. Your call," he says, sliding his jeans on and standing.

"Ugh. Deal," I say, sticking out my bottom lip in a pout. He leans forward, capturing my lip in his teeth and pulling gently. My pulse jumps like a car going from zero to sixty in two point five. I don't want him to stop, ever. But like all good things in life, even this must come to an end.

He releases my lip, and I pull it into my mouth, nursing the swollen, bruised edge. "Good. Now let's go handle these horses," he says, swatting me on the ass.

"Okay," I say, meanwhile thinking about pulling him back to the corner and stripping his clothes from his body with nothing but my teeth. He bends at my feet, and for a second, I think he's going to torture me with kisses along my legs, but he picks something up off the ground.

It takes a few seconds longer than I'm proud to admit before I realize he's stuffing my panties into the front pocket of his jeans.

I follow behind him, snapping a few more pics of his delicious backside before putting the camera away and getting started on our day. There was still a lot I needed to learn about the way the ranch ran and the people who worked to make it run efficiently in order to find other things we could add to make it better.

"Have you ever thought of offering horse riding lessons?"

"Sure. It makes sense to offer something like that, but getting word out would be hard. I couldn't ever justify the cost of hiring someone to give lessons unless we had a steady stream of interested people."

"Yeah. Good point." But now I'm here, and if I'm good at anything, it's bringing the crowd in.

"Who would you have teach them?"

"I don't know. I guess I could, for now. Why, do you think we should start offering some?"

"I think it's a good idea," I say, and then because I want to help, "I gave a few lessons back home. I wouldn't mind helping if you need it."

"What other ideas do you have?" Well, at least he didn't shoot me straight down. That's gotta be good for something, right?

"Aside from lessons, I think we can offer trail rides. Beginner, intermediate, and advanced. Tying into the trail riding, I think we can offer a wedding and party venue. We could even promote some local artists once a month or something. Support each other and build each other up."

"I like it. But I'm not planning a damn wedding."

"Obviously. We would just offer the venue and maybe a horse-led carriage ride to the altar or something."

"People pay for that shit?"

"Hell, yeah. But that would just be the fun, simple stuff. I'm playing around with a bigger idea, but I haven't worked out all the kinks yet."

"Let me know when you do. I'd like to hear it."

"Sure." I copy his earlier response, trying not to show my excitement. When Beau and I discussed how Calvin was likely to react to my reappearance, he didn't hold back. I knew I had hurt Calvin by leaving, but until Beau laid it out for me, I didn't realize how badly. It put the pain I felt when he hadn't followed me in perspective.

I had been prepared to fight him on every change. To argue and push and demand that he listen. I don't think either of us expected him to be quite so amicable. Not that I was complaining at all.

Add in the sweet ache between my legs, and I'm willing to accept that maybe we were wrong. Maybe, just maybe, Calvin Hunt is as ready to put the past behind him as the rest of us.

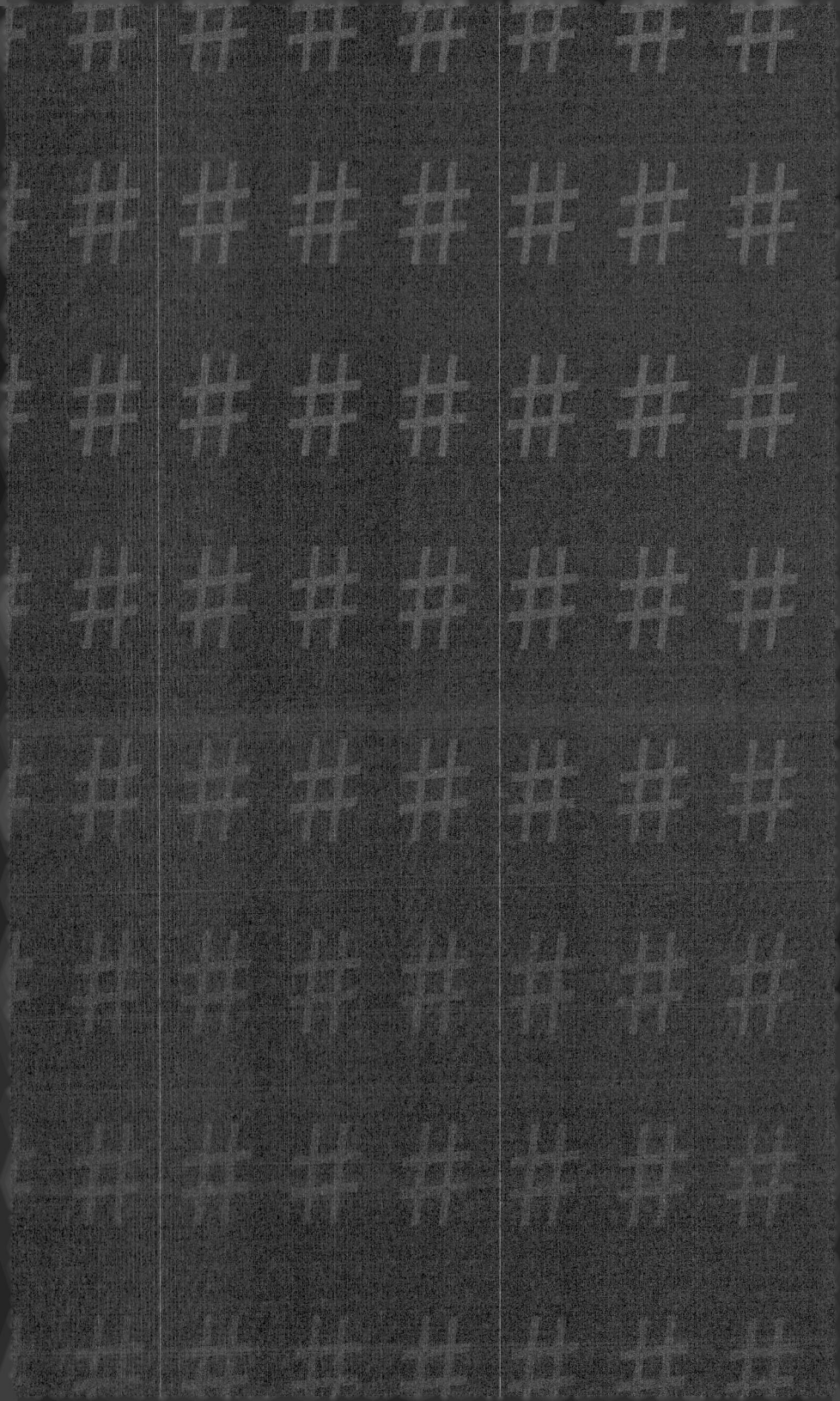

CHAPTER TEN

#just fun

Calvin

I SPENT that and every day following by Blake's side, working on her plan to revamp this place. We worked well together, and if I couldn't keep my eyes off her, well, who could really blame me?

We've managed to keep our hands mostly to ourselves since falling into each other's arms the day of the photo shoot, not that I didn't think about undressing her and having my way with her every second of the day. Her presence is intoxicating.

I don't know what brought her back to Alabama, but every day she's here, I thank God while secretly praying she doesn't leave again. I'm torturing myself. I should ask her plans, but that feels too much like something a boyfriend would do.

She's made it abundantly clear that she isn't looking for

anything like that, and truth be told, I'm not either. We have sex. Only sex. It was bound to happen, given our past and the chemistry between us, but that didn't mean we couldn't move past it, couldn't be friends too.

I could move past it.

Shit happens.

"I like that," I say, leaning across her, my arms rubbing against her own. We've been working on the layout and photos for the website she's creating for PRR. I didn't know shit about any of it, but I like being close to her.

"Yeah? Like this, or . . ." She clicks a few buttons and the picture morphs into something else. "This?" Her face turns toward mine, her lips inches from mine. I lean down, pressing my mouth to hers.

"That one. Definitely that one," I say, kissing her.

Okay, so maybe I hadn't gotten enough of her yet. But I was working on it. "Mmm. I like that one too."

I have a feeling neither of us is talking about the pictures. I reach for her waist and spin her so she's facing me. Her ass is pressed against the kitchen counter, her hands gripping it white-knuckled.

"Lift," I instruct as I work to unbutton her jeans. She places her palms flat and pushes away from the counter as I peel them off, panties included. She glances at the door, worry creasing her brow.

"The door is locked. No one will come in," I reassure her.

"I wasn't worried." I recognize the core of her voice, but those words are so full of sex and need that she sounds like a different woman. She sits naked before me against the cold counter, completely at my mercy, open and fucking beautiful.

She watches my hands caress the curves of her body,

smoothing along her waist to her hips, down her thighs, and back up again. I raise my eyes to hers and then lift her onto the counter. I spread her legs wide, one hand on each knee. My lips graze the flesh from the dip of her stomach, over her hips, and across the sensitive skin between her legs. I nip the inside of her thigh and then press my lips to the spot, kissing away any pain before moving to another area. I take my time torturing her, never quite arriving at the center of the bullseye where her body screams for me.

With each pass from one leg to the other, I come closer and closer to her begging center. The breath of my exhale dances across her clit. She sucks in a breath, waiting, anticipating, but I stop short of ecstasy only to repeat the torture over and over until she's cross-eyed, breathless, and soaking wet, desperate for release without my ever touching her there.

"You're so wet for me, Blake," I say right before dipping two fingers into her folds. She gasps, and I reach around to her ass with my free hand to pull her to the edge.

"Ahh, Cal . . ." She sighs, forced to lie back and support her upper body with her elbows. I bow my head between her legs and press my lips to her center in a gentle kiss before flicking my tongue against her, setting every nerve ending below her waist on fire. I lick her clit, circling it and suckling it between my lips in a passionate kiss.

I curl two fingers inside her, lifting her hips with the erotic tempo. Gasping between pants, she instinctively clamps her legs on either side of my head, but I gently repeat the process of spreading her legs with her knees, opening her wide and giving a little sharp jerk that clearly says *don't move*. She grips my hair tightly as I alternate between circling her clit and licking her outer folds. I pull my fingers free and reach down, pulling my cock free of my jeans. I'm swollen, hard as a rock, and want nothing more than to bury myself deep inside her. I pump my hand up and down my cock while sucking her into my mouth.

"Oh, fuck, fuck, fuck." She lies back and tilts her head, watching my arm pump below the countertop edge. "Stroke your cock for me, baby." I moan against her on the verge of exploding. "Fuck, that's hot. Shit, Cal. I'm going to come."

She thrusts her hips forward, offering more of herself to me, her orgasm building quickly with every electrifying movement of my tongue. She's close. I can feel it. "Oh, shit." Her hand grips my hair, holding my face against her center. I pump into my hand faster and faster until my balls tighten and the first wave of pleasure courses through me.

"Oh, God, Calvin," she yells, her body convulsing violently. I ease back when she relaxes her grip on my hair. Blake props up on her elbows and looks up at me through her beautiful long eyelashes. Her face is relaxed, her eyes glazed in the after-orgasm glow. I grab a towel from the basket on the counter and wipe my hand, then, leaning forward, I press a soft kiss against the inside of her thigh.

"I've wanted to do that since I heard you in Beau's kitchen that morning."

"Shit. Why did you wait so long?" she says, taking her clothes from my outstretched hand.

"Anticipation makes for a welcomed distraction."

"I see," she says, grinning. "So, you like the first picture?"

Laughter bubbles deep and full, erupting before I have the chance to stop it.

CHAPTER ELEVEN

#blessyourheart

Blake

I'VE BEEN BACK in my hometown for weeks, and during that time, I've come up with ten different ways to avoid answering the same questions from nosy do-gooders in town.

"Well, color me pink. Is that you, Blakelynn Smith? I haven't seen you since graduation. What's brought you back to little ol' Greentown, Alabama?"

I turn at my name being called and then wish I hadn't. I would recognize the bleached blonde locks and sunless tanned skin of Jessica Mink if she was on the cover of *Where's Waldo* with 100 more of her dressed just the same. We were friends in high school. Or rather, we were two of the sixteen kids in Greentown's graduating class. When you grow up in a town the size of Greentown, you don't choose your friends. Even if you wanted to, there weren't enough of them to pick between, so everyone was friends with everyone else and there wasn't a secret to share in town.

I can't say I missed her when I left. Truth is, up until I saw her again, I hadn't even remembered her. I'm not sure if that makes me a horrible person or not. Probably does. I should add it to the list of things I'm trying to work on.

"Jessica. How are you?" Beau and Calvin choose that moment to walk up, thank God. Maybe I can get out of here before I turn gray. I raise my eyes and beg Beau to help me escape, but judging by the light dancing in his blue eyes, he doesn't plan on helping.

"Married. Got two kids now, seven and four. You and that sexy as sin fiancé of yours planning on starting your family right away? I bet you're excited to finally have a ring on that finger. You're a little behind, but you always did do things in your own time."

My gaze snaps to Calvin, who sucks in a deep breath. I wasn't sure if he knew I had been engaged. It's safe to say he didn't.

"Hey, Blake, we've gotta get back. You ready?" Beau takes pity on me and rescues me after all. I owe him a cold one for that. Later.

"Gotta go, Jess. We'll catch up later, okay?" I say and take off on Calvin's heels.

We pile into the cab of the truck together and head back to PRR. A short trip into town for feed turned disastrous fast. Things had finally settled between Cal and me, even if I was secretly stripping him in my mind every time I looked his way. I was allowed to think about another man. Just because my fiancé cheated on me and we split in the last four months didn't mean I had to pretend to be dead. I could look. And I could enjoy what I saw. And if the opportunity arose for me to touch some of what I saw, then there was no harm in that.

When we pull into the drive, Beau bails and leaves us to unload the feed. Tension's thick enough to cut with a knife, and after the third time he passes me mumbling under his breath, I lose it.

"What?" I yell, dropping my bag on the ground and twisting toward him.

"I didn't say anything to you."

"No, you're mumbling under your breath. If you have something to say, then spit it out."

"I don't." He takes a step past me and then changes his mind. "You're engaged? What the hell are you even doing here, and don't give me that bullshit excuse that you're here to help PRR because we both know that's not it."

"I'm here for PRR. My personal life it just that. Mine."

"You didn't think I should know? We're working together twelve to fourteen hours a day. And fucking another hour or two on top of that." He's inches from me now. I could reach out and touch him if I wanted, but now he's pissed me off, and I let the anger roll through me.

"No, I don't think I owe you a damn thing. Least of all, a play by play on my life since the last time I saw you, but since you want one, here it is. I left. I moved on. I've had lovers and relationships. One of those lasted three years before he decided to ask me to marry him, and I said yes. I am allowed to be happy. I'm sorry that the happiness I found wasn't in your arms."

I can tell my words sting. And for a second, I feel bad.

"You think I care that you moved on? News flash, Sugar. I

did too. I'm not mad about the fact that you had lovers. I'm pissed because for the last week, you have been tearing my clothes off every chance you get." He takes a step closer. Our bodies are a breath away from touching.

I can't breathe. He's sucked the oxygen out of the air itself, and at this moment, I don't even care. I just want him to lean down and press his lips to mine. I want to taste his mouth against mine. My eyes follow my train of thought, and I lick my lips before glancing back at him. Instead of kissing me, he takes a step back. "And then I find out you're fucking engaged. I don't know what the hell happened to you, but the Blake I knew wouldn't be thinking about one man while promising to marry another. She damn sure wouldn't be fucking him every chance she got."

With that, he leaves the barn and I fall to the ground and fight the tears clogging my throat. It's not that his words hurt me, more that they infuriate me. I clench my fist and take a deep breath, pulling it in through my nostrils and then pushing it out through clenched teeth. My temper has always gotten me into trouble. I've spent years trying to control it, but if that time has taught me anything, it's that I should keep my mouth shut when I'm pissed. My words tend to cut like knives when I want them to.

Cal has no reason to not assume I'm exactly the person he described. I've hidden the truth of many things from him since coming here. I try to remind myself of that when the desire to hunt him down and cut into him burns through me.

CHAPTER TWELVE

#letsride

Calvin

WHEN I PULL up to the ranch the next day, Blake is already outside with that devil of a horse, Samson. She's got her phone out and attached to a long pole and is talking out loud while walking around the horse. I cringe when she steps behind him, sure he's going to kick her, but he stands perfectly still and lets her do whatever she wants.

I walk as close as I dare to hear her.

Samson is just one of the many horses here at Point of Retreat Ranch. You can follow his story by searching the hashtag Samsonthebigbaby. Starting next week, I will be back each morning with a new guest, but for today, I wanted to catch everyone up and let you know about the changes in my own life. Like Samson here . . .

I walk away. I don't need to hear what she's been up to, and I damn sure don't want to hear about the picture-perfect life she's building. I know yesterday, I yelled at her about making googly eyes while being engaged, but the truth is if she didn't make the first move in my direction, I would have. I damn sure didn't stop to ask if she had someone at home. It took everything I had in me to walk away when I did.

Before we headed into town yesterday, we all sat down and mapped out the first phase of Blake's plan for PRR. She was convinced we needed to bring the place to social media. Right now, you could look up the phone number in the *White Pages*, but that was it. I personally thought that was enough, but like Beau pointed out, I wasn't the professional.

"Ready?" Blake asks, stepping into the tack room. So far, the only conversation we've had has revolved around work and PRR. I wasn't ready to hear about her life or listen to her make excuses for her actions. My Blake is gone. She proved that.

"Sure. What do you need me to do?"

"I'd like to take a ride and mark a few different trails. A simple one first and then a couple more advanced. I've got plastic ties to mark them."

"Sounds good. I'll start saddling up the horses. I hope you don't plan on taking that beast."

"Why not? He would be fine, but no. I thought I'd take sweet Annie today." *Did she really ask why not? I don't want to see you tossed to high heaven, how about that?* I don't say any of that, though. After yesterday, I'm trying to keep the number of words I let out in her presence to a minimum.

"Do you still remember how to ride?" I don't mean to sound like an ass, but aside from her love life and the fact that she gave a few lessons, I don't know what she has been doing the last decade.

"I'll manage."

Thirty minutes later, Blake is tying the saddle bag on Annie's saddle, and after checking the girth, she lunges onto her back. I open the gate and let them exit before walking a bay gelding named Spark out and shutting the gate.

We head northwest, away from the cattle pasture. She leads the way like she knows exactly where she wants to go. Every once in a while, she will lean out of the saddle and tie a piece of blue plastic string to a tree. I try not to stare at her ass when she leans over.

Try and fail.

Our first trail takes about an hour and a half to mark. I imagine the time would be cut down to around forty-five minutes if we weren't stopping every few feet. The path she cut is a simple one, but scenic, leading down the creek's edge before turning back and returning to the beginning of the trail.

When we stop and let the horses have a drink, she offers me a bottle of water from the saddlebag. I search my mind for something safe to talk about but come up empty.

"Do you want to do the hard trail next or something intermediate?"

"Whichever you think is best." Not what I was expecting. Now that I think about it, she has been more agreeable than normal.

"I have a good idea for the harder trail, although I don't know how we're going to get these cleared in time to start offering them before the fall."

"I've got Greentown High sending students here to volunteer as part of their elective studies. There are several groups who are looking for work to spice up their college applications."

"Oh. That's a good idea."

"You sound surprised. I do have good ideas. This one included. I know you think it's stupid and a waste of time, but this is going to work."

"I don't think it's stupid. I just don't understand how posting something somewhere online is going to bring people to the ranch." I shake my head at the ridiculous idea.

"There's a little more to it than that. I'd be happy to show you if you're ever curious enough to learn." With that, she pulls the reins and leads Annie back down the path toward the barn, letting her have her head. I kick Spark gently to pick up the pace. Eleven years ago, I would have picked Blake into a race. We would have laughed the whole way back before falling into each other's arms. Then I would have kissed the laugh away until something else burned in her eyes.

But she belongs to another man now. And I'm over her.

Of course, Spark let me know exactly what he thought about that when he lifted his tail and let one rip.

CHAPTER THIRTEEN

#regrets

Blake

I REALIZED three things sitting on the dusty floor of the barn after Calvin ripped into me yesterday.

One. He thought I was the worst kind of cheating piece of shit. And I hated that.

He viewed me the way I viewed Brad. And that sucked ass.

Two. I wanted Calvin Hunt. And not just as a partner in this new business venture. I wanted him the way I hadn't wanted something since I was eighteen and couldn't think past leaving this town and starting my life. I wanted him on a fundamental level I wasn't sure I even understood yet, but the thought that he saw me as someone who could break a promise like marriage vows or anything else really bothered me.

I hadn't figured out how to explain the situation yet. Not

without making him also feel like I had lied to him about being engaged. The entire time we hung flags, I was trying to find a way to broach the subject, but nothing sounded good in my head.

Oh, hey, Calvin. You know when you said I was stripping you with my eyes? It's because my body is craving your touch.

Oh, yeah, Calvin. I forgot to mention that fiancé I was talking about . . . well, he doesn't exist.

Hey, Cal, I'm so pathetic at relationships that my fiancé decided to sleep with my best friend.

Nothing worked.

And three, I am the biggest damn idiot this side of the Mississippi. I could have set him straight yesterday, but instead, I let my temper get in my way. I had a thing about men assuming the worst of women, and in this instance, he really had the right.

Before I know it, we're done and the sun is setting. We've spoken fewer than ten sentences to one another, and I could cry from disappointment.

"I'll unsaddle the horses and brush them down. It's been a long day. I'm sure you're tired," Calvin offers, and I nod, sliding from the saddle.

After tying Annie off, I head toward the house, but instead of taking a shower and relaxing, I grab a six-pack of beer from the fridge and head back to the barn. Calvin's already got the saddles off both horses when I make it back. I turn the corner and run straight into him. He's taken his shirt off, and every single muscled line of perfection is on display.

I trip over my own feet trying to back away, and he reaches out to steady me. My skin tingles where his fingers grip my arm. I hold up the beer as an explanation since I can't seem to speak, and he grins. I swear to God, my body temperature rises ten degrees with that smile. Calvin takes the six-pack from me and sets it on a hay bale, pulling two free. He twists the tops off, passing me one.

I pull a horse blanket off the stall door and lay it across the hay bale before sitting down. I'm going to have this conversation whether it kills me or not.

"I wanted to talk."

Calvin's brow raises, but he doesn't reply.

Suck it up, buttercup, and spit it out.

Honestly, I've never been the type of girl who's afraid to speak. I usually have too much to say. I'm the most opinionated person I know, and it's a struggle on most days to keep my mouth shut until someone asks for my opinion. I lost plenty of friends before I learned that.

Hell, I made a career out of talking to people. Of sharing my life with people. The good and the bad, the pretty and the ugly. I realize now that I've done my followers a disservice by backing away while I deal with my own drama. They come to me with all of their ugly. I owe them the truth of my own. I decide to record about it tomorrow.

To bare it all.

But first, I need to tell Calvin.

CHAPTER FOURTEEN

#noregrets

Calvin

"I THINK there was a misunderstanding somewhere, and I should've cleared it up as soon as I realized it, but honestly, I let my anger get in the way. For that, I hope you can forgive me." Blake stands and starts pacing. I remember she did this when she was younger, too, any time she needed to work out a problem or say something important, so I let her pace and I wait.

"When you yelled at me about eye fucking you, you were right. I'm sorry about that, by the way." Definitely didn't expect this conversation.

"Its fine, Blake. I shouldn't have—"

"No, let me finish," she says, and I clamp my mouth shut. "I didn't expect you to find out about Brad that way."

When I raise my brow, she understands. "Brad is the fiancé. But that's not what I meant, either. I didn't expect anyone to know about him, and I guess that's my fault. I mean, I put everything online for the world, so of course, people knew, but I guess I didn't expect someone from back home to care enough to be following me."

"So, you're sorry someone let the cat out of the bag? Sorry you got caught?"

"No. No. I don't care about that."

"I don't understand, Blake. What are you trying to say?"

"When I came here, or when I decided to come back here, it was so I could get away. I needed space and I needed to find myself again, I think."

"Okay . . . so things aren't perfect," I say, trying to follow her zigzagging conversation.

"Yes. I mean no. Fuck, why is this so damn hard?"

"Brad was sleeping with my best friend."

I take a step closer to her, invading her personal space.

"What are you saying?" I ask. I need to be sure. I need to hear the words from her mouth.

"I don't have a fiancé. I have no one. I wasn't cheating on my person. I don't have a person."

I crush my mouth to hers, pulling her closer until her body is melded to my own. Her lips part, and my tongue dives inside, teasing her own. She tastes like watermelon and sunshine. I don't want to ever let her go.

I could kiss her for hours. Days, even. But one of the horse's neighs breaks through, and we separate, breathing heavily. She laughs a little and leans in to wrap her arms around my neck. Her lips touch mine as light as a feather, and then she kisses the side of my mouth, my cheek, and down my neck before finding my lips again. Her own lips are smiling.

"I was afraid you would be mad."

"Why the hell would I be mad? I've wanted to do that since I saw you standing in Beau's kitchen."

"I thought you might feel like I had lied to you, which, so we're clear, was never my intention."

I take her hand, and together, we finish tending to the horses. For the first time since she arrived, the conversation flows freely. It finally feels like my Blake is back.

CHAPTER FIFTEEN

#teenagelove

Blake

WHEN I WAKE the next morning, it's with a smile on my face. I lie in the bed and remember the night before. We didn't do anything other than kiss, but it was perfect. I felt like a teen again, making out with my boyfriend. We finished the six-pack and then lay in the front yard, staring at the stars.

Calvin wanted to know all about the last decade of my life, and it felt good to fill him in. I promised to show him some of my work today after I got the new website for PRR up and running. He didn't have any social media accounts, so trying to explain how the posts work was difficult.

I get dressed and make my way downstairs. It's become a daily habit to meet Beau for coffee before starting our day.

When I walk in the door, Calvin is already there. I grin, passing him to get my own cup and humming while I pour cream. When I turn back around, Beau is looking at me like I've grown three heads.

"What?" I ask, taking a seat at the table.

Beau glances from me to Calvin and back to me before slapping his hand on the table. "Well I'll be. What do we have here?"

"I don't know what you're talking about," Calvin replies, and I smile.

"What?" I ask again.

Beau stands pointing at first me and then Cal. "I see what's happening here. I see it and I like it," he says, pouring himself another cup.

I toss back my head and laugh. Leave it to Beau to call the nail on its head. It's one of the things I love the most about him. He doesn't bullshit anyone. If he has something to say, he says it. Period.

"I think I like it too," I say on my way out the door.

I'm going live this morning again with my Instagram, but this time, I plan on letting my followers know what's been going on. It's going to be a hard video to film, but after clearing the air with Calvin, I feel better about it. Either way, I plan to give them my truth. But first, I want to spend some time with Samson.

I've been wanting to talk with Beau about Samson. He has done so well here that it's got me thinking about how we could help other horses in similar situations. Up until now, the ranch has mostly only boarded horses, but this fall, we will start offering riding lessons and trail rides. It would be amazing to add a rehabilitation program to the ranch as well.

I've read amazing things on the uses of essential oils in aromatherapy for horses and equine interactive massage. Both of which I think would benefit a number of horses that have been hurt and traumatized from injury or even abuse. It would take a while to get it up and running, and someone would need to be hired to run the program, but I only know of one other similar program, and it's in southern California. There's nothing on the East Coast.

It's one of those things that would set PRR apart from all the competition.

I saddle Samson and walk him to the hitch post. He prances back and forth, excited. It's been almost five months since I rode him, and I can feel the energy pulsing off him in waves. I check his girth and bridle before unlatching the lead line from his bridle, then I climb onto his back. He takes off before I'm fully settled. I ease my boot into the stirrup and gather the reins. Calvin steps out of the house as we pass.

"Shit, Blake. Wait," he calls, and I toss back my head laughing, letting Samson run.

We fly across the pasture, cutting ground. My hair whips around my head wild and free. I let him run until we near the creek and then pull him to a trot. When we reach the end of the easy trail Calvin and I marked, we cross the creek and slow climb the hills. The view takes my breath away.

I can see for miles. A low fog hangs to the treetops, a sign of fall coming. Golden hues of light mix with blues of the sky and spread across the eastern skyline. Birds call to their mates in a symphony that would rival the greatest artist.

Another string loosens from within. I've missed this, its pure and welcoming embrace. In Arizona, the mountains are bare and the fields all clay. The colors are just as amazing, but in a different way. This feels like life. Arizona feels like the past. I know at some point, I will go back, but I don't think I will ever call it home again.

Samson paws at the ground while I take in the surrounding beauty. I wonder how it feels for him to be safe and loved. I reach down and stroke his neck. Hooves beat into the earth behind us, and I know without looking that it's Calvin. I expected him to follow me, still scared that big, bad Samson will hurt me.

I wait for him to join us. It doesn't take long. Spark is breathing heavily, and Calvin's gaze searches my body frantically.

"Took you long enough," I say, and he relaxes.

"Well, you had a head start."

I laugh. It feels good to laugh again. I wasn't sure that I would ever want to again. Alabama has been good to me, healing.

"What were you thinking, racing off on that beast? He could have killed you."

I spin Samson around to face Cal. He's now beside Spark, and other than a quick sniff of the snout, he doesn't show a care in the world. Calvin tenses, waiting for the horse to attack, but he doesn't know Samson the way I do.

"Samson isn't going to hurt me. He trusts me."

"You don't know that."

"Yes I do. We've worked together a lot since I rescued him. He can be scary, but we're working on that, aren't we, Sammy?"

"Rescued him? You're his owner? Beau told me it was some chick out west, but I never . . . rescued him from what?"

"We think he was abused when he wouldn't cooperate. By

some hotshot man with a complex. He wanted a trophy horse and knew next to nothing about how to care for a fish, much less a horse. He's terrified of men, but he's working on overcoming his fears. That's why Beau had him here. I needed someone I could trust to work with him."

"Beau doesn't work with the horses. He's the cattle man."

"I know." I wait for that to sink in for him. I knew Beau wouldn't have much time with Samson. He told me that himself the times he visited Arizona, but Calvin would, and there was no one I trusted more with him.

Even twenty years ago, as a child of ten or eleven, Calvin had been a horse person. I grew up watching him work with them, ride them, and care for them. He has always had a gentle heart and a caring soul. Samson was in good hands.

"I had no idea."

"You've done a good job."

"Why didn't you tell me he was yours? I've been losing my mind every time you step next to him."

"Honestly, I was afraid you would turn him away."

He doesn't reply. I think we both know that before I came back, that is exactly what Calvin would have done. He didn't want anything to do with me or anything that was a part of me. All those years ago, I didn't think of what it would do to Cal for me to leave. We grew up together, best friends since kindergarten, maybe even earlier. Cal's mom had been best friends with my mom.

We spent entire summers together, swimming in creeks, riding horses, and chasing cows. It wasn't until high school that things changed, the way they usually do. We went from best friends to lovers overnight. I never hid my dreams from Cal. He knew I wanted out. I wanted as far from this town as my car would carry me. The last night of my seventeenth year, just before the strike of midnight, Cal helped load my Toyota down, and when the hour changed, I left and never looked back.

Anytime I thought of Cal, it brought up memories of my mother, and I didn't want to think of her. I didn't want to remember the pain that came with losing her.

"What are you thinking about?" Cal asks.

"My mom. Would you believe I can't even remember the last time I thought of her? It's like I blocked her out altogether. Ran as far away from her memory as I could."

"You needed the time away. Losing her took something from you."

"Yeah. It did."

"How's your mom?" I ask.

"She's good. Been wondering when you would be stopping by."

"We should do that soon, but first, race you back to the barn," I say, tapping Samson in the side. He takes off like a rocket, flying along the path until we need to descend. I let him find his own pace, trusting him to get us down safely. Calvin is right on our tail. He's never been one for losing.

When we reach the bottom, I urge Samson faster, pulling ahead. I round the bend and see the barn come into view, but something else has me pulling hard on the reins.

Sitting in front of the barn doors is a Red Camaro.

Calvin races around the bend and almost rides straight into us, but he manages to stop in time.

"What is it?" he asks, following my line of sight. I turn to him, my eyes frantic.

"It's Brad."

I barely get the words out before he takes off, heading straight for the barn.

"Shit. Shit. Shit. Come on, Sammy, let's go." I'm not worried about seeing Brad. I couldn't care less about that, but I am worried about how Cal is going to react to his being here, and if his taking off is any indicator, we are in for a day from hell.

I jump off Sam's back before we're even fully stopped and loop the reins across the hitch. Calvin is a few feet from Brad, fists clenching.

"Calvin, stop. Let me handle this."

To my surprise, he stops, turns to me, and then changes direction, storming across the yard to Beau's. I can't begin to describe the look in his eyes, but my stomach drops regardless. I'll hear all about it later.

Brad is leaning against the driver's door. He's dressed in slacks and a white button-down, with the sleeves rolled up his forearms. He's every bit the attractive specimen he was when we first started seeing each other, and yet, I feel nothing for him now. No butterflies in my stomach, no anger at his cheating ass. Nothing.

"Friend of yours?"

"What the hell do you want, Brad?"

"No hello? How are you? Did this place suck all the manners out of you?"

"Nope. I just don't have the time to waste on you. Now what the hell do you want?"

"I miss you."

"I'm sorry. That must be hard. Maybe Cindy can help."

"I'm done with Cindy. It was a mistake. I missed you so much, and you were always busy with the company. You never had time for me." That stings, mostly because I said the same thing to myself when I first caught him, trying to justify his actions.

"So, let me get this straight. You miss me so you sleep with my best friend? How does that make sense to you?"

"I fucked up, Blake. I know I fucked up. There is no excuse for it. I know that. But I don't want to lose you over one mistake."

"I . . . I don't know what to say, Brad. I made my decision when I left."

"But you can change your mind. Don't throw away almost four years, Blake, please. Just think about it. I'll be in town for as long as it takes. I don't want to lose you."

I don't answer him. I can't. And before I find the words to string together, he's pulling away. On one hand, I understand what he's saying. Four years is a long investment to throw away. If I were coaching another couple prior to having experienced the betrayal myself, I would urge them to try. I would tell them they owed it to themselves.

After the heart-wrenching truth settled into my gut the day I heard Brad and Cindy, I didn't think I could ever see his face without hearing those noises again. And now he shows up, wanting to make things work.

"What the hell, Sammy? Can you believe this shit?" I loosen the girth and slide the saddle and blanket off his back. Steam rises from his sweat-soaked skin. I lay the saddle across one of the stall doors and grab a wash bucket and brush.

One of the first lessons you're taught when riding is that afterward, you let the horse cool. No food or water until their body temp levels back out. Otherwise, you run the risk of a horse colicking. I've only seen one horse colic, and it was more than enough for me. Essentially, a horse lacks the ability to throw up, and if it eats while hot, the stomach and intestines can twist, causing gas to build up. Most don't survive it.

I let Samson cool while I unsaddle Spark and then pull the water hose out. Starting at his feet, I coat his skin, cooling his body, and then lather up and wash every inch of him before rinsing again. I comb out his mane and tail and braid them both in long, thick braids. While I work, I go through the situation with Brad. In my heart, I know I can't make it work, and not because he slept with my best friend.

I started dating Brad because he was the type of man I thought I needed. He looked the part. He never pushed me in anything. If I needed to leave for a week or a month, he would be there when I returned and everything would continue like no time had passed. I was comfortable, complacent. Being with Brad was like taking the next step on the imaginary ladder I had created in my mind. The ladder I needed to reach in order to finally consider myself a success. But it was shallow and empty.

Our relationship lacked everything that made a relationship worth fighting for. It lacked fire and passion, and while I did care for him, I don't think I was ever truly in love with Brad. He stepped in and filled an empty slot in my life, and I let him stay because he didn't disrupt it.

When I finish with Samson, I've made a decision about Brad. He can hang around town until he starts speaking with a southern accent, but I'm not going back to him. After unhooking Samson, I lead him to his stall and then do the same with Spark. The West Coast should be waking up about now, and I have some things I need to get off my chest.

Grabbing a water from the fridge, I make my way to where I set up this morning. It's time to update my followers and let the pieces fall where they may.

CHAPTER SIXTEEN

#ihatered

Calvin

SITTING in the house while Blake stood outside talking to the piece of shit who cheated on her almost drove me crazy. As soon as his car careened out of the drive, I jumped in my Ford and left. I needed a minute away so I didn't open my mouth and say something I knew I would regret.

I listened for screaming and yelling, but all I heard was silence. Other than the shocked expression when she saw his car, she didn't seem the least bit upset that he was here. She didn't seem upset with him at all.

I wasn't sure what to make of that. I thought after last night, she was done with him. At least, that is what I was led to believe. I didn't think Blake was the type of person to play games and string someone along, but I hadn't seen her in over ten years. People change. I knew that better than most.

I drive down Main Street when I see his car at our local watering hole and U-turn into a parking space out front.

The bar is dimly lit, Keith Urban bellowing from the speakers. There is only a handful of people inside, but even if it had been slammed, I would have been able to pick him out. City slickers never really fit in, no matter how hard they try. Brad didn't try at all.

I slide into the bar a couple of stools down and wait for Janie to pass me a Bud Light. He's managed to start conversation with a couple of locals, and I listen to him bullshit his way through a few conversations.

"Can you believe it?" I don't register Janie until she sets my beer down.

"Believe what?"

"He came all the way down here to be with our Blake. What a love story. I hear they're supposed to be planning a wedding, may even have it down over on Blackberry Lane."

"Who told you that?" I ask with more bite than I intend, and Janie takes a step back. She glances at Brad and back to me.

"Oh, Calvin, I'm sorry."

I stand and toss a five on the bar without touching my beer. So she decided to take him back? After everything he did to her? I slam the door to my truck and back out. I thought last night meant something. I knew there were some women who'd run around, kissing on people and doing all sorts of other things without a thought in the world about a future, but I didn't think Blake was like that. I thought we shared something special. Hell, truth be told, I thought she was back and that we'd finally have our chance.

I let her go eleven years ago because I knew that's what she needed. She had always wanted to see the world and live in a big city where no one knew her. I wanted her to experience that life. So when the time came, I helped her pack her bags and load her car. I didn't ask her to stay, not that I thought she'd be able to, anyway. I let her go, and I spent the next few years avoiding every trace of conversation about her. I wanted great things for her, but I didn't want to hear about them. It tore my chest open imagining her out there without me.

After a while, I gave up the idea of her ever coming back to me. Maybe what I had felt for her was different than what she felt for me. I accepted that I had lost my best friend. I had lost the love of my life. For the next five years, I worked my ass off. When Jim, Beau's dad, passed away, leaving the ranch to him, he asked me to come on board as a partner. We'd split everything 50/50, including the debt his dad left behind. I didn't have anything else, so I accepted and poured myself into PRR. For the last year, we've worked to build Point of Retreat into a respectable cattle ranch and boarding facility, month after month, slowly paying off past debts.

I finally had something of my own. It wouldn't ever replace the love I felt for Blake, but it gave my mind something to focus on other than what we had.

I never expected to see her again. I had given up the idea. I'm surprised I didn't fall on my ass when I saw her standing in Beau's kitchen. For a minute, I thought I was hallucinating.

Everything happens for a reason. I believe that. I've tried to live by that, but I'll be damned if I can find a reason for her showing up and then leaving with the piece of shit who hurt her. I just can't. I refuse to sit by and watch her walk away from me again. My heart can't handle it.

CHAPTER SEVENTEEN

#missinglover

Blake

I SEARCH for Calvin after going live. I want to celebrate new beginnings and fresh starts.

What's Cal's number? I text Beau. He sends me the contact followed by a question mark.

I thought he was with you.

Brad showed up and Cal took off.

Shit.

I close out of our messages and open a new one, adding in Cal's contact information.

Hey, it's Blake.

Where are you?

Wanna grab dinner?

I send three messages, back to back. It's a weird quirk of

mine, but I never text long messages. I send thoughts as they occur to me, and usually, they're too sporadic to be part of one message. It used to annoy Brad to death.

I check the responses to my live video online and am surprised by the numbers. Not only that, but the number of comments wanting to know about where I am and what's happening here. I hadn't thought much about promoting PRR to my personal followers, and now I wonder why. It would be great for both of us, and if done right, I could get a jump on Point of Retreat's social media presence.

With that thought in mind, I head inside.

Four hours later, I've got Point of Retreat online on Instagram and Facebook and put the final touches on the website. I've put in an order for business flyers and posters to hang around town and created a newsletter to keep subscribers updated about changes and upcoming events.

I still haven't heard back from Calvin, so I text him again.

Hey. I want to show you something. Then I send the link to the website.

When he doesn't text back again, I head downstairs to see if Beau is still up. He is, and from the smell of things, his stomach led him to the kitchen. I knock on the back door and step inside.

"Hey, you hungry? I was just whipping up some breakfast for dinner."

"I'm starving. I messaged Cal earlier to see if he wanted to grab dinner, but I never heard back."

"Hmm. You said Brad was here. Did Cal see him?"

"Yeah, but he wasn't here long. Cal went inside so I could deal with him, and next thing I know, he's gone. You haven't heard from him?"

"No, but I haven't tried, either."

"Oh."

"Listen, I don't mean this the wrong way, but if you plan to work things out with Brad, then maybe you should give Cal some space. It's not going to be easy for him to lose you again."

"Why the hell would I work things out with Brad?"

"You're not?"

"No. What makes you say that? Is that what Cal thinks too? Is that why he's ignoring me?"

"I don't know, Blake. As far as how I knew that, well, I'd ask Brad. Seems he was a bit talkative at Joe's, and his story doesn't much match yours."

"That weaseling son of a bitch. I'm going to kill him."

"Maybe stop short of murder?"

I pile my plate with eggs and bacon and pull two pancakes on there too. I'm gonna need my energy for when I find Brad.

"The asshole could have talked to me. He didn't have to run off."

"Yeah, but look at it from his point of view."

"I am. Which is why I'm not planning to kill him too."

Beau laughs, and some of the tension in the room fades away.

"Probably just kick his ass real good," I say, shoving a bite of syrup-filled pancakes into my mouth.

"Want me to record it?" Beau asks, and the rest of the tension leaves. I nod, swallowing, and take a drink of water. The rest of dinner passes in comfortable silence. I send the link to the website to Beau and let him open it up on his phone.

"Do you see anything you want changed?"

"Blake, this is perfection. I wouldn't change a thing."

"Awesome. We'll put the final touches on the trail ride

schedule, and then we need to start interviewing for a horse lesson trainer. I can do it until we get someone in here, since I doubt we'll have a lot of interest in the beginning."

"Okay. I can let Janie down at Joe's know and put up a flyer at the feed store."

"Sure. Sounds good. Let me know if you want me to post online, but I think finding someone local would be best, if possible."

"Agreed."

I rinse my plate and load the dishwasher with our dishes.

"I'll see you in the morning. Thanks for dinner."

"Goodnight."

I shower and climb into bed, but before setting my alarm, I check to see if Calvin has texted.

He hasn't.

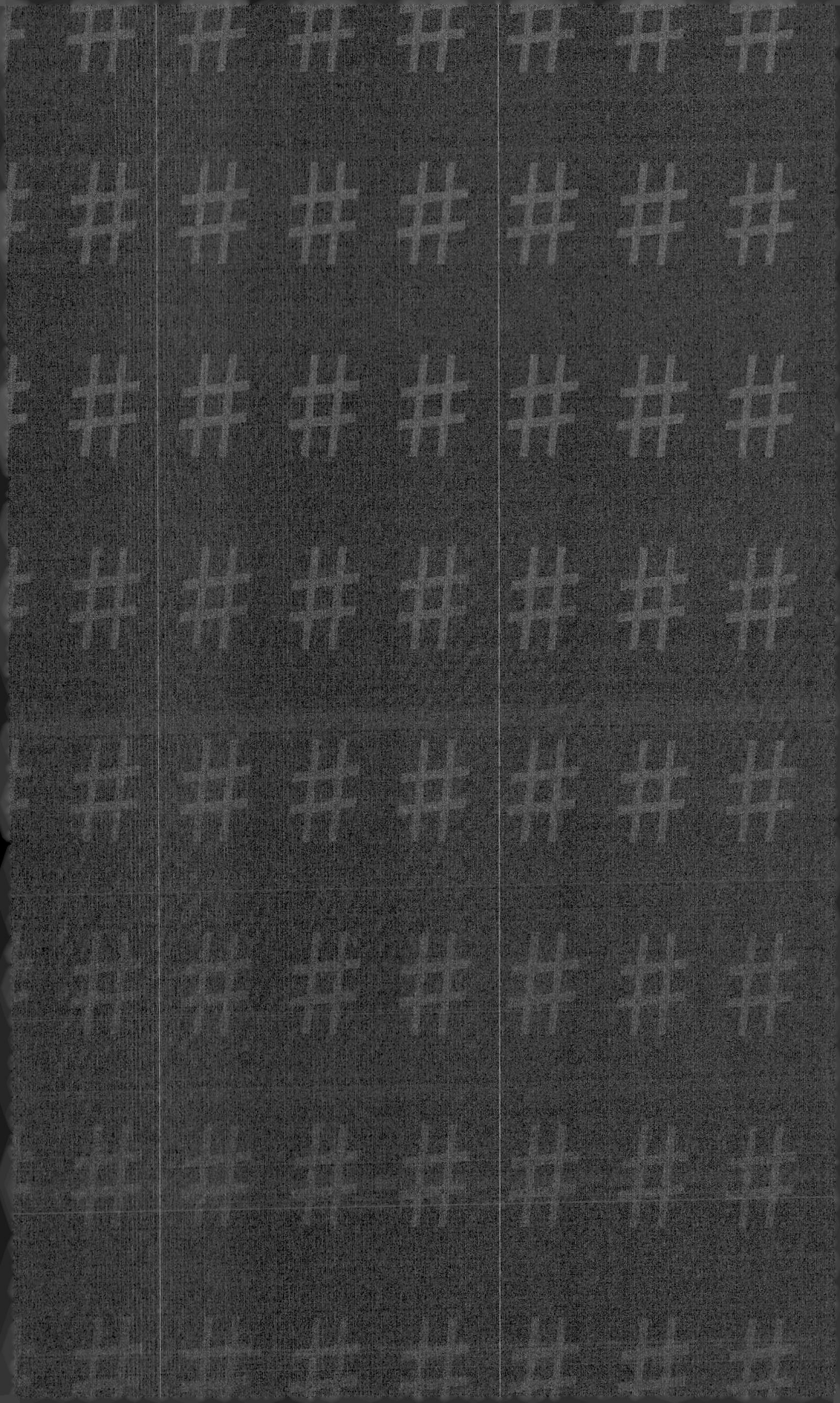

CHAPTER EIGHTTEEN
#rinseandrepeat

Calvin

THE THOUGHT of seeing Blake with Brad makes my skin crawl. If she can't see that she deserves more, I don't know how to open her eyes.

In order to avoid Blake, I'm also avoiding Beau and the ranch. At least until she leaves, then I'll go back and attempt to pick up the pieces she leaves behind.

When she first arrived, I didn't put much stock in her ideas on expanding, but once she explained it all to me, I could see it taking off. The closest registered horse trainer is over a hundred miles away, and I don't think he offers lessons of any kind. A lot of people want to experience the fun of riding but haven't grown up doing it the way I had, and without someone there to teach them the ins and outs, they wouldn't ever get the chance.

Blake is offering them that opportunity. Hopefully, she wouldn't be mad if we decided to continue it without her. Maybe I could talk Beau into asking her.

"Calvin, phone," Katherine, my mother, called from the living room. Yeah, I ran home to my mother's. It was the only place where I knew Blake wouldn't find me. She hadn't been able to see my mother since her own had passed away. I think in a lot of ways, my mom reminded her of exactly what she'd lost. It didn't help that Mom and Tricia, her mom, were so close. Through all of Tricia's appointments and treatments, my mother was there. Seeing her would bring back stuff Blake had been running from for years.

"Yeah?" I ask, picking up the phone receiver.

"Calvin, did you forget how to answer your damn cell?"

"No. I left it at the barn and haven't been back to get it yet."

"Do you plan to come back anytime soon?"

"Is Blake still there?"

"Yes."

"Then no."

"Calvin, listen—"

I cut him off. "Let me know when she's gone. Gotta go." I hang up and turn off the ringer. Mom will be pissed when she realizes it, but I don't wanna hear any of Beau's shit right now. Mom has a list of odds and ends around the house that need done, so I pull it from the fridge and get started.

Two hours later, I've changed three light bulbs, tightened the bathroom faucet valve, flushed the water heater, and replaced one of the stovetop coils. I'm only a fourth of the way down the list. I open the fridge and grab a bottle of water then add another item to the list, *replace fridge light*, when I hear the sound of a truck pulling up.

Figuring it's Beau come to give me a piece of his mind for not answering the phone, I step outside. Sure enough, his truck comes barreling down the drive, but Beau isn't inside.

"You have to be the most irritating jackass I've ever laid eyes on." She's wearing a sundress that cuts off mid-thigh with her damn cowboy boots. My mouth goes dry at the sight, but as fine as she is, I'm not in the mood to hear more bullshit from her.

"What do you want, Blake?" I ask, taking two steps at a time. I didn't want to do this. The last thing I want to do is fight with her. I'd rather remember her galloping across the field, the wind in her hair and that beast of a horse under her, but she's here now, and from the look of things, she's here to fight.

"What do I want? Funny you should ask that now, after taking off and ignoring my calls."

"I haven't ignored you. I don't have my phone."

She marches across the yard and stabs a finger in my chest. "But you did leave."

"Don't you have somewhere else to be? Something else to be doing?" I ask.

"Yeah, I've got something else I want to be doing." Grabbing my shirt in her fist, she pulls my face down and presses her lips against mine. I'm too shocked to pull away, and truth be told, I wouldn't even if I could.

"Stupid. Arrogant. Prickly ass. Man." She mumbles each word between kisses.

"What the hell are you doing?"

"I'm kissing you, dumbass. Wasn't that obvious?"

"But Brad—"

"I don't want Brad, dummy. I want you."

Never in a million years did I think I would hear those words. "But Janie said—"

"I know what Janie said. She told me when I stopped by there looking for you. I don't know why Brad is going around saying the shit he is, but I'm never taking him back. I should have never said yes to marrying him to begin with. I guess I thought that's what I was supposed to do. I don't know."

"So, you're not planning your wedding and leaving us all again?"

"And let you destroy all of my hard work? Pshh. Not a chance. Now take me inside to see your mama. It's been too long."

She doesn't have to tell me twice. Mom is in the kitchen when we walk in, and as soon as she sees Blake, her eyes fill with tears. Blake curls into her arms the same way she did as a kid, and for the longest time, they just hold each other. When they separate, tears are streaming down both of their faces and the back of my throat is burning, but I'm pretty sure it's just from all the dust in the air.

"You're the spitting image of your mama, baby girl."

"Yes, ma'am. I've heard that a lot."

"I miss her too, baby." Blake nods, unable to speak, and Mom pulls her back in for another hug.

"I'm sorry I stayed away. I just . . ."

"I know. You're back now. That's all that matters. Are you planning on staying?"

I hold my breath, afraid of her answer. Her eyes search the room for me and hold mine for a fraction of a second before she nods. "I plan on it."

"Good. This is home. Good."

For the first time since seeing Blake again, I take a deep

breath and let it fill my lungs. I've been worried about getting too close to her or letting her back in my heart for fear of her running right back out the door. A part of me didn't believe she was home to stay but was too scared to ask her myself.

"Who's hungry? I'll fire up the grill and make some burgers."

"I can make the patties," Blake offers, making herself right at home. Mom eyes her for a second and then winks at me. Her face says it all. I haven't seen her this happy in a very long time.

"I'll whip together some potato salad if you wanna toss some corn on the grill too, Cal."

CHAPTER NINETEEN

#catchingup

Blake

AFTER DINNER, I help clean up the kitchen and kiss Katherine goodbye. I won't let as much time pass before coming back. I know now that my leaving had been a mistake. I was terrified of seeing her, thinking that being around her would hurt too much, but it was the opposite. She reminded me of the sweet times we had before Mama got sick. I needed this, even if I didn't know I needed it.

Calvin walks me back out to Beau's truck and kisses me again before shutting the door.

"You staying here tonight?" I ask.

"I suppose."

"Okay."

"You gonna be able to find your way out here on your

own?" We both know I could drive this road blindfolded, but I don't say that.

"I might need some help. It's been a while."

"I could drive you back, if you want?" he offers, running his hand across my exposed knee.

"Would you mind?" I ask demurely.

"Slide over."

He climbs in the cab of the truck with me and starts the engine. The headlights cut across the lawn as he circles around and heads down the drive. I try to focus on the road, on the stars in the night sky, on the bobble head dancing on the hood, but my mind is stuck on Cal. Sliding across the seat, I curl under his arm and lay my head against him.

I let my hand fall to his thigh, and then, when he lays his arm across my shoulder, I start to draw small circles along his thigh, up, up, up, and then down, down, down. His breath turns shallow and my heart skips into overdrive. Tilting back, I place my lips on his neck and kiss him there light as a feather, then again higher along his jaw.

"Fuck, Blake. You're gonna make me wreck this damn truck."

"Pull over."

He steers the truck to the shoulder of the road and shoves the gear shift into park. I kick off my shoes and crawl into his lap, my hands pulling at his belt buckle before I've even fully settled. I don't know what's come over me, but declaring to him that I wanted him, not Brad and not anyone else, has left me vulnerable and aching for him in a way I don't know how to describe.

His warm chocolate eyes gaze up at me, and he blinks slowly once . . . twice. I have no idea what he's thinking. No clue what he's searching my face for. Then his mouth crushes to mine, and I don't think at all. I let my instincts lead me to touch him, feel him. When he lays me on the seat of the truck and slides into me, I fall apart in his arms. My body convulses, shattering around him with an intensity that takes my breath away. Afterward, I pull my dress back down and curl back into his arms where I stay for the rest of the drive home.

CHAPTER TWENTY

#sorrybeau

Calvin

"BEAU IS GOING TO KILL ME," Blake says, giggling. She's so fucking perfect I don't know how I've lived without her.

"Nah."

"You don't understand. When I asked to borrow the truck, he specifically said, 'As long as you don't plan to have sex in it.'"

"Oh, damn."

"In my defense, I didn't plan anything. It just happened. Right?"

"You should have been a lawyer. You're pretty good at finding loopholes."

I cut the lights when we pull in the driveway and coast the

truck to the front yard. I climb out the passenger side and meet her at the hood.

"Come up with me?" she asks.

I don't reply, choosing to grab her hand and lead her upstairs instead. I toss my boots inside the door and watch Blake pull the dress over her head and toss it on the couch.

"I need a shower. Feel free to join me."

She doesn't have to ask me twice. I've spent the last ten years wanting her. Anytime she offers, I will show.

She's already in when I undress and make my way to the shower. Steam billows, filling the bathroom and blocking my ability to see more than a few feet in front of me.

I step into the spray of water, letting it wash away sweat and nastiness from the day. Reaching for a loofa, I squirt some body wash and latter it until bubbles are falling from it, then I run it along Blake's shoulder, down her arms, and back up, repeating with the next arm. Then I drop the luffa and use my hands on her stomach and chest, liking the way her skin feels beneath my hands. Soft and smooth.

My cock hardens again, and this time, she drops to her knees and spends an ungodly length of time torturing me with her sweet mouth. It takes all of my strength to not come.

I can't get enough of her. It's like my body is hell-bent on making up for lost time. As long as she is willing, I don't see a problem with it. When we fall into the bed later that night, she's asleep before her head hits the pillow. I lie next to her, trailing my fingers up and down her naked body, praying she meant what she said earlier.

I didn't want to hope, didn't want to give her the chance to crush me again, but the heart wants what the heart wants, and mine has always wanted her.

CHAPTER TWENTY ONE

#sweetandsore

Blake

WHEN I WAKE the next morning, it's to the most exquisite soreness I've felt in a long time. I roll over and pat the bed, searching for Calvin, but the bed is empty and cold where the night before, it dipped with the weight of his body.

I sit up and look around the room, searching. My eyes see a note folded across the pillow. Opening it, I smile and fall back.

Good morning, beautiful. Went to feed the horses. See you soon (:

I climb from the bed and slide on a pair of jeans. I don't know the last time I ran through bathroom business so fast, but I'm in a hurry to get outside and not just because I want to see Calvin.

Today, I'm going live and showing off some more of the

ranch. Since I got the website up and running yesterday, I'll be able to tag PRR in my video and hopefully drive some traffic to the site. With a little bit of luck, we'll have steady traffic coming through by the beginning of next month. We still need to hire a few people, one for lessons and a couple to give rides along the trails, but until we know what kind of reaction there will be, it's hard to justify that expense.

Calvin is bent over scooping feed into a bucket when I walk in. I stand by the door, admiring his fine toned ass until he straightens, turning toward me. Samson neighs, and I pull some loose hay from a bale and pass it to him, giving him the love he wants.

"That horse has you wrapped."

"You're just jealous."

"Damn straight, I am. He's already got two kisses from you. Meanwhile, I'm over here working my ass off and got none."

"Poor baby," I say, stepping to him and wrapping my arms around his neck.

"'Bout fucking time." I didn't even hear Beau come in. I was so caught up in the moment with Calvin. I blush and Calvin pulls me closer. Slapping his chest, I make him release me.

"What do we have planned today, Boss Lady?"

"You with us today?"

"Yeah, I've got Billy checking the cows, so I'm all yours. Do you need me to do anything?"

"Yes. This is great. I'd love to introduce you and Cal today when I bring up the ranch. I think it would be good to put a face to a name for the followers."

"Sounds good to me."

"Sweet. I'm gonna let Samson out for a little while, but I'll hunt you down before I start the video."

"Hunt us down. I'm stealing this one from you for a few, if that's all right?"

"Yeah, no problem." I grab a lead line and hook it to Samson's halter before unlatching his stall door. He's more than ready to get outside and tries to pull ahead of me, but I hold him to a steady pace.

He runs in circles when I release him into the pasture, kicking his hind legs up. You'd think he was never allowed out with the way he acts, but I let him play almost every day. Silly horse.

While Samson plays, I set up my laptop and get everything ready to go online. I grab my phone to see if Shelly had called yet and see six missed calls and a dozen missed texts from Brad. I open the messages first and read through them.

I miss you.

Wyd?

I tap the message box and type out a message for him. I should have already handled this, but truthfully, I was more concerned with finding Cal and righting that wrong than I was with Brad.

Me: We should talk. I'll meet you at Joe's tonight at 8.

He texts right back like he's been sitting waiting for my reply. I almost feel bad, but I shake it off.

Brad: I can't wait to see you.

Me: 8:00

With that handled, I call Shelly and check in. Our daily check-in has become every few days since I've been gone. She's handling things fine without me there dictating every move, and I'm starting to realize how much of a control freak I was. It's nice to step back and know everything's still being taken care of. I'm not ready to turn over the reins completely, but taking a step back and letting the staff I had handpicked do the job I'd chosen them for is a nice change of pace.

With business handled, I check the time and head back in the house to find something to put in my stomach. Skipping coffee and breakfast didn't sit well. Lucky for me, Beau went to the store a few days ago and I'm able to snag a blueberry muffin and banana off the counter.

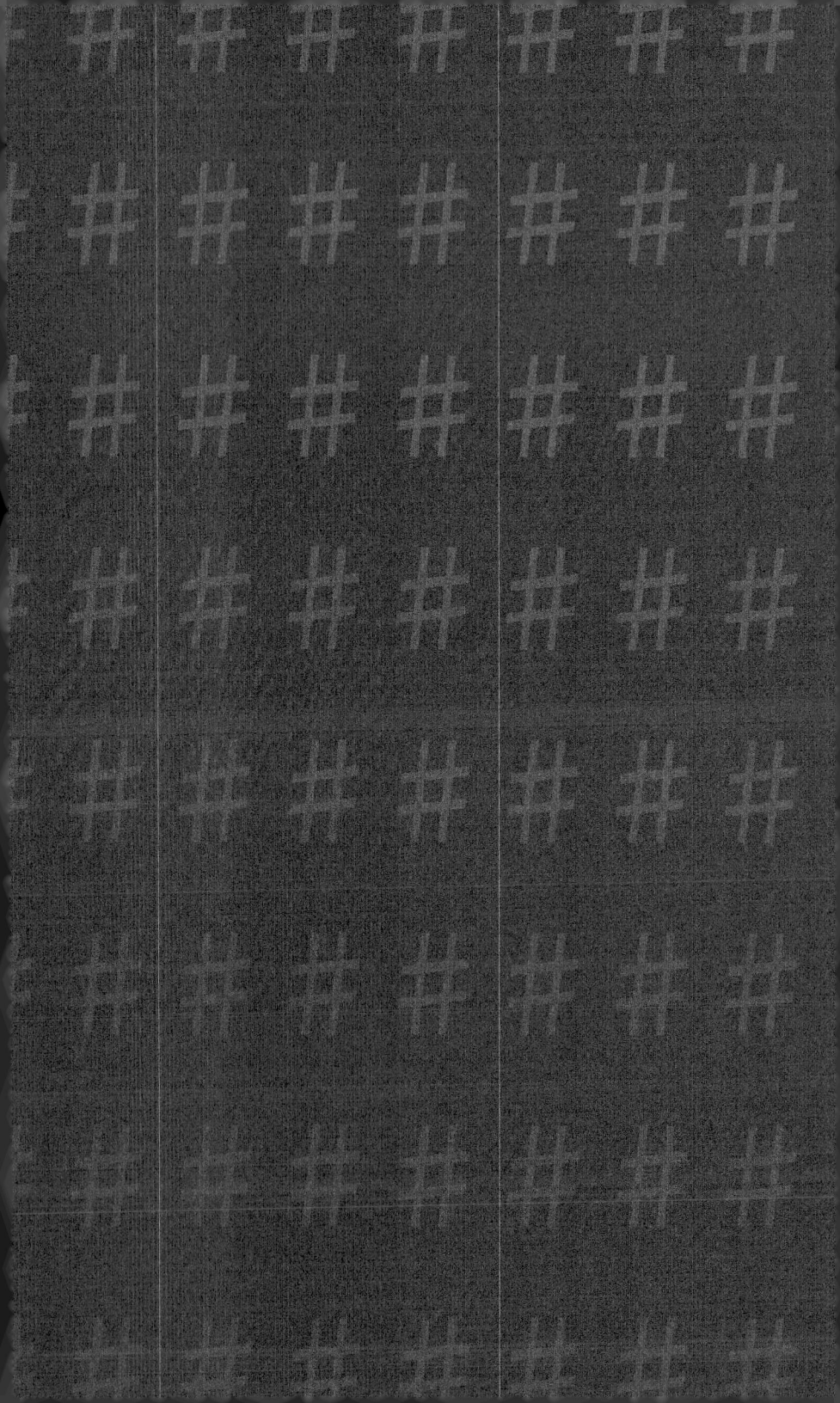

CHAPTER TWENTY TWO

#hardtalk

Calvin

BEAU DOESN'T ACTUALLY NEED help with anything. A fact I discover about five minutes after leaving Blake. He dragged me away on the pretense of work so he could give me the third degree on Blake.

"What are you doing, Cal?"

"What do you mean? I'm helping you with an imaginary project."

"Stop the shit. You know what I mean. That girl has been through hell recently, and you need to be sure you're in this for the right reasons before jumping headfirst."

"You think I don't know that? Oh, that's right. You kept up with her so you think you know her better? I know what she's been through. I'm not adding more shit to her plate."

"Aren't you, though? Running off, leaving her without a word. Is that your way of paying her back for leaving you?"

"Fuck you, Beau. You know me better than that."

"I thought I did. But then I never would have expected you to leave her high and dry either."

"I fucked up. I know that. I thought she was going back to that fuck wad and I didn't want to see it happen. I couldn't watch her walk away again."

"I know what you were thinking. Hell, I know why you were thinking it, but that still doesn't make your actions okay."

"I know. I won't leave her again. I don't care what happens. I won't hurt her."

"Make sure you don't. You and Blake, y'all had something, and hell, maybe you can again, but that girl is like a sister to me and I'll be damned if I see her hurt, even if you are my best friend."

"I love her, Beau. I always have. Fuck, I think I always will. Even if she up and left me again right this second, I'd still love her."

"Maybe try not to let her run off again."

"She can run if she wants, but this time, I'll be chasing her."

"Good. Now that's out of the way, let's track this crazy chick down and see if we can't sell the hell out of this new idea of hers."

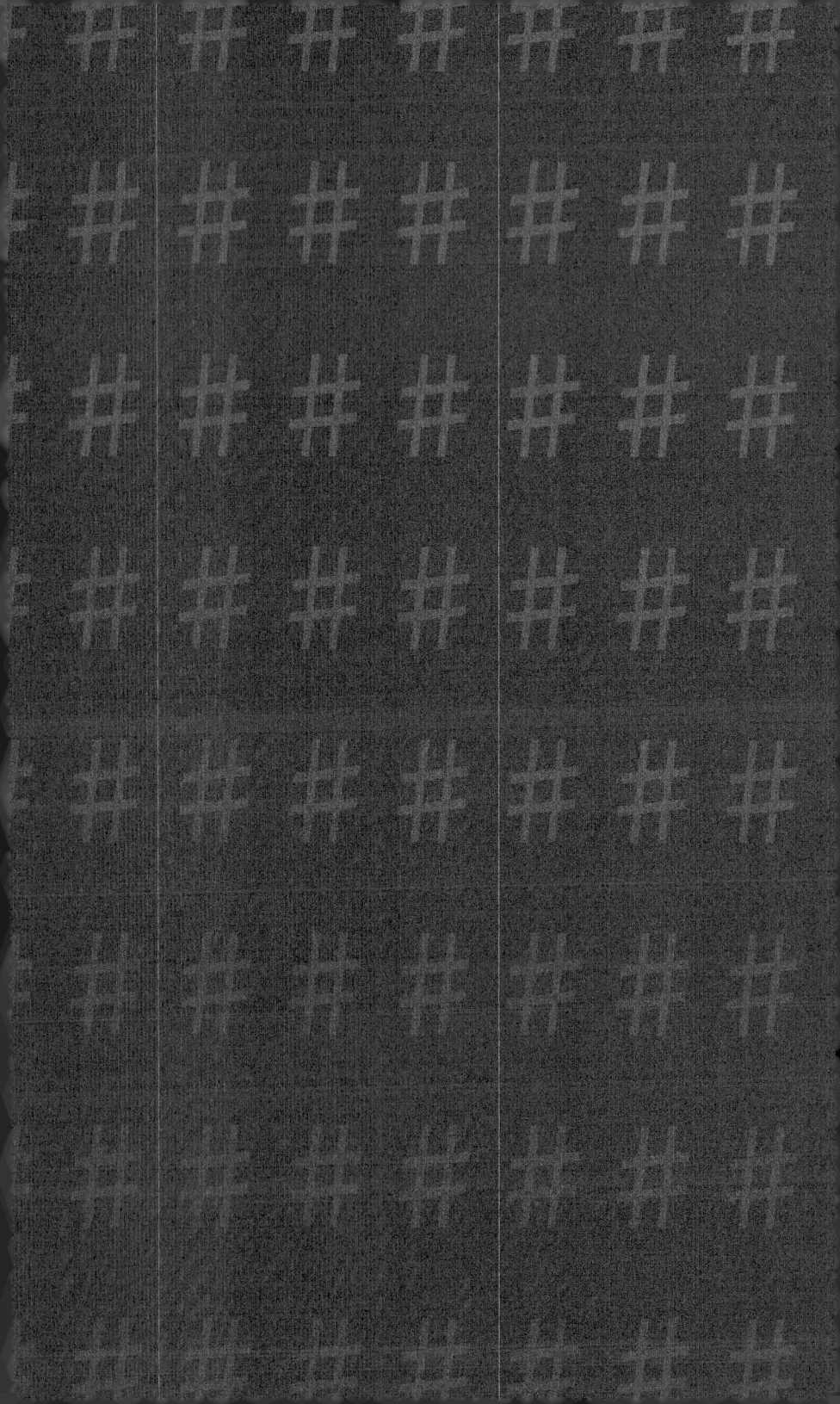

CHAPTER TWENTY THREE

#hesmine

Blake

THE GUYS WERE A HIT. I mean a HIT. I thought I would have a hard time building up the following for PRR, but after getting a look at the two sexy as sin men running the place, the comments section filled faster than I could keep up with.

The website already had over three thousand subscribers and was steadily climbing.

"Were going to need to look into hiring some people sooner rather than later."

"You think so?" Beau asks.

"Um, yeah. I've got over a hundred people wanting lessons and at least double that interested in um . . . rides." I cough a little, reading a particularly interesting comment asking whether Beau was available for personal ride. I don't think she meant on a horse, either.

"I'll stop by and post the flyer this afternoon. Should swing by and let Marcy know the hotel might see some customers here soon."

"Good idea."

"Actually, I think I'll head there now. Unless you need me for something else?"

"Nope. I think I'm good here," I say, scrolling through the comments. Some of this shit makes me want to blush. But the ones about Cal have my hackles raising. I want to reply, *Sorry, ladies, that one is mine,* but things are so fresh and new with him I don't even know what the hell you would call us. I know I'm happy and I want to be with him. I shouldn't be feeling that way yet. Especially after ending my relationship with Brad less than four months ago, but the heart wants what it wants.

The problem is, I don't know how serious he wants us to be, and until I do, I can't stake a claim. No matter how badly I want to.

"What's got that crease popping up between your brows?" Calvin asks, leaning over my shoulder. When he sees the comments, he pulls my phone from my hand.

"What's this? *Calvin can pull a whip on me anytime he likes. Calvin can take me for a ride anywhere.* Are you jealous, Sugar?"

"No. I just don't like the thought of you guys being objectified. Now give me my phone back so I can delete the comments."

"Uh-uh. I know the green monster when I see him. And right now, he's eating you alive."

"Shut up." I reach for my phone, jumping on my tiptoes, but he holds it just out of my reach.

"Let me see if I can figure out how to work this thing," he says, clicking the *Image* button. The camera opens facing us, and he pulls me in for a kiss that leaves my toes curled in my boots.

"There. Problem solved." I open the app and look for the photo he took. He caught the kiss perfectly. And then I see the caption.

Sorry, ladies. He's taken.

My heart swells until I think it might burst from my chest. I guess that answers my question. We are officially together. Instagram official, even. I toss my phone to the side and jump into his arms, wrapping my legs around his waist. I kiss him.

"Speaking of jealousy, I wanted to let you know I'm meeting Brad later." He pulls back. I can tell he's trying to decide how to respond. I might find it funny if I hadn't just been about to delete my whole account to keep from seeing lustful comments about him. And those women hadn't ever even met him. I was *engaged* to Brad.

"He's been texting and calling. I told him I would meet him at eight tonight. I need to lay it out for him now that the pain and shock of catching him have faded. he's hanging on to the idea of an us, but there isn't one. I just thought it would be better to tell him in person. That way, he can't claim that he misunderstood."

By the time I finish explaining it to him, he's nodding in understanding. "Then I was thinking you could buy me a drink and we could make it Greentown official too."

"Yeah? You want me to tag along with you?"

"Of course. I mean, I'll talk to Brad alone. There's no

reason to ruffle feathers or rub us in his face. I'm not trying to be mean or hateful."

"I'll stay at the bar, and I won't interfere at all unless he steps out of line, then all bets are off."

"Deal." With that handled, I head inside to freshen up.

CHAPTER TWENTY FOUR

#Thisguyagain

Calvin

BRAD IS WAITING for her when we walk in. I head straight for the bar and don't look back. She wants to handle this on her own, and I plan to let her. The last thing I want is for her to think I'm some overbearing ass who can't trust her.

Joe's is busier than usual for a Thursday night. The bar is just about full, but I find a seat at the end where I can watch Blake without it being obvious.

"Beer, Cal?" Janie asks, and I nod, pulling out my wallet. "Why don't you gimme a shot of Jack with it too?" She pulls the bottle from the back wall and tilts it into a fresh glass.

"Want a bite to eat?" she asks, reaching for the menu. I shake my head.

"Nah. I'm okay right now," I say and glance to where Blake is sitting.

"Damn, what's happening over there?"

I shrug. Even knowing, I'm not one to pass around other people's business. Janie watches them for a minute before having her attention pulled to another customer. I take a sip of my beer and then toss back the shot.

Brad grips Blake's hand, and even from here I can see the pleading look on his face. I don't blame him for begging. Hell, if I thought I was about to lose her, I'd be on my hands and knees, begging. What he doesn't know, and I'm sure she isn't telling him, is that Blake couldn't marry him even if he hadn't decided to sleep with her best friend.

Eleven years ago, she ran from this town as fast as her car would take her. Running from the pain and heartache losing her mom had caused and chasing dreams bigger than even she could comprehend. She took everything she owned and piled it in that car, but she left her heart here.

Maybe she wouldn't have ever realized it if he hadn't shaken her beliefs to the core, but I'd like to believe she would have. She'd been sending pieces of herself back for months before she caught him. First with that damn brute of a horse and then with her ideas. Whether she knew it or not, she was coming home. Brad just gave her a nice swift kick in the ass.

"You want another?" Janie asks, stepping back by. "Yeah, I think so, but pour me two glasses."

"Two? You got company coming?" she asks at the same time Brad stands, kicking his chair back under the table. Blake doesn't even flinch. She stands and tells him goodbye and then meets my gaze.

"No. She's already here." I see the moment it clicks for her and then she pierces the air with a whistle.

"Hell, yeah."

I pass Blake her glass of whisky and grab my own, offering a cheer.

"What are we toasting to?" she asks.

"Greentown official," I say and tilt my shot back and then pull her in for a tongue torching kiss. The bar erupts in applause, and I shake my head at them while Blake tries and fails to hide her blush.

CHAPTER TWENTY FIVE

#roadTrip

Calvin

I WAKE Blake early the next morning by kissing up the inside of her thigh. She scoots up the bed, trying to get away, but I pull her leg, yanking her back down the bed, and press my lips to hers.

"Cal," she moans into my mouth breathlessly.

"I'm about to head out, baby."

"No." Her hands bunch in the fabric of my shirt and she pulls me down across her. "Stay with me."

"Damn you, woman."

"I need you," she whimpers, her hand running down my stomach and across the zipper of my jeans. I planned to be on the road half an hour ago, but the warmth of her body next to mine kept me hostage in the sheets. "Ugh, I hate horses," she groans, pulling her pillow over her head.

"Liar," I say, peeling it away and capturing her lips.

She kicks the comforter off her legs and then wraps them around my back, locking them together and refusing to let me go. The kiss deepens and my hips flex involuntarily against her.

Last night was the most amazing night of my life. I want to spend every night for the rest of my life making love to Blake. Learning her body, her curves. I want to memorize every inch of her and spend an eternity worshiping her body. She is exquisite, the most beautiful thing I've ever set eyes on, and she is mine.

I don't deserve her.

But I will spend forever trying to.

With that thought in mind, I peel the nighty over her head and flick my tongue against her taut nipple. She moans, pressing her chest toward my warm mouth. I suckle one and then the other, not wanting to neglect either, and then I stand, leaving the softness of her arms. She whimpers, reaching out a hand, and I smile. My little vixen can't get enough of me, either. I kick off my boots, followed shortly by my pants and boxers, then I climb back into the bed on my knees. I nudge her legs, and they fall open, ready and waiting.

"Look at me, beautiful. Let me see your eyes."

She opens her eyes, gazing at me with lust-filled pools of desire and need. I line the head of my cock up with her slick slit and shove into her with a single push. Her breath hitches, followed by a contented sigh, but I want more. I want to hear her scream my name. I want to be the one and only thought she's able to have. Every time she moves, every ache she feels while I'm gone, I want to remind her of me, of this.

I slide from her hot, wet opening slowly, teasing her along the way, and then I shove back into her hard and fast. My pelvis slams against her clit over and over until I feel her tightening around me and I know she's close, ready to explode. I grab her legs, setting them on my shoulders, and pull her ass closer to me and then, holding her hips, I slam into her harder, deeper, faster.

"Oh, fuck, fuck." Her walls clench around me, and with no other choice but to join her, we spiral together, her convulsing around me and my cock pulsing, shooting, filling her. Her legs fall from my shoulders, and I slump forward. I don't know if I'll ever be able to move again, but I've got places to be and people to see. Sliding from her, I stand on shaky legs. She rolls, tucking a pillow to her side, and within seconds passes back out. I make my way to the bathroom and clean up, then I slide back into my pants and lean forward, kissing her temple before walking out the door.

CHAPTER TWENTY SIX

#makingamends

Blake

THE DRIVE to Katherine's is bumpy. Her house sits at the end of a long dirt road. Every few feet, there's another pothole the size of Texas. I clamp my teeth tight to keep from biting my tongue as I bounce my way along. I take it slow, trying my best not to destroy Beau's alignment along the way.

When I mentioned wanting to stop back by and see Katherine, Beau offered me his truck again. We both knew there was no way in hell my little bitty Malibu would make it down this drive, and Cal was still gone delivering Billie to a woman named Samantha. I could have made the drive with him, but we are less than three weeks away from opening day at PRR, and I'm going to need every second I can squeeze out of the day to have it ready by then. So far, only one investor has signed on, leaving me to pick and choose which programs to add right now. It's a lot of number crunching and even more around the table discussions, but I'm satisfied with the way things are lining up.

After a six-hundred-year journey down the drive, I finally arrive at Katherine's. The last time I was here, I didn't pay attention to anything other than where Calvin was hiding. We had another miscommunication and he went into hiding, not that I blamed him at all. She's painted the whitewashed shutters a bright red sometime during the last decade and added on to the porch. It wraps around the entire house now, covered in plants and rockers. Mom would love it. Their favorite thing to do was to sit outside and rock back and forth while catching each other up on town gossip.

I can almost picture them there now.

"Well, to what do I owe this lovely surprise?" Katherine asks, meeting me on the porch. I don't know what led me to visit today, but the thought wouldn't leave. It buried itself deep in the recess of my mind, and every time I tried to start something new, the idea, sorta like a mosquito, would reemerge until I couldn't bat it away any longer.

"Hey, Katherine, how are you?"

"Oh, pish, don't act all formal with me, girl. Come here and give me a hug."

I lean into her and soak in all the love I've been denying myself. Katherine had been a second mother to me. She and my mom were both left raising children alone for whatever reason, so they buckled down together. I never felt the absence of my father. I was surrounded by people I knew loved and cared for me. At least until I'd decided to leave, never once thinking about how that would make someone else feel.

"I'm so sorry, Katherine," I say, finally realizing why I felt the need to come here.

"For what, daughter? What's wrong?"

"Nothing. Not now. I'm sorry for leaving and cutting ties with everyone back home, especially you."

"Oh, pish. You needed to get away. I understood that. And you came back, just like I always knew you would."

"You did?"

"Of course. Alabama clay runs in your blood, girl. You can leave, but this place will always draw you back."

"It's home."

"Yes, it is. Now how about we head inside? I just pulled a peach cobbler from the oven."

We spend the next few hours catching up. I tell her about my company and how I'm not sure what to do with it now. I spent years building it into something that I could be proud of, and I am so proud. But my heart isn't in Arizona or LA or any other city. It's right here in sweet home, Alabama.

"It's not Calvin, either. I mean, part of it is, but what we have is so new. We're relearning each other, and maybe it will work out, but either way, I want to be here."

"Can you not do your work from here?" she asks, and I pause before answering.

"I can. I can do a lot of it from here. But there's so much more that I have no desire to do, like traveling on a whim. I can still consult. That wouldn't be an issue."

"Well, why don't you hire someone to do the rest? It sounds like you can afford it, right?"

"Yeah. Yeah, I can." It's not the first time I've thought about it, either. It makes sense, in a way, but it keeps me in the loop more than I want. I don't need another employee under me with whom I have to follow up and check in on. I need someone I can pass the reins to. Someone I trust to not run the entire thing into the ground.

When I hug Katherine goodbye, it's with a fuller heart and a calmer mind. I might not know what to do with my business or my life, but I've started mending a bridge I didn't mean to break. I couldn't imagine the ups and downs of having a child. It flat out terrifies me.

The sun is starting to set as I make my way back down the drive. There were a thousand things I should have been doing at home, including finding a place to live permanently, but seeing Katherine was what I needed for my soul. Something dings in the truck, and I search the dash for the cause. The low fuel light is lit in neon orange. I debate stopping but in the end figure it's the least I can do since Beau loaned me his ride. I pull into the gas station and pop the lid before sticking the pump in. It's still strange to pump my gas before paying, but in a small town, I guess if someone raced off without paying, they wouldn't get very far. Everyone knew everyone here, and the last thing you wanted was the preacher teaching about theft on Sunday morning because you stole gas.

I click the pump so it can fill up and head in the store.

"Can you not tell me where the turn off is, sir? It's imperative that I reach Miss Smith as soon as possible." My ears perk when I hear my name. I glance to see who is working the register and smile when I see Harry behind the counter. He raises his brow and shrugs his shoulder like 'Outsiders. What do you do?' I chuckle under my breath while checking the coolers.

"I've already been by the barn, and some gentleman there told me she was at this Katherine's house along with directions

THE WAY WE LOVED

on how to get there, but I don't know where the tree that burned last spring is so I can't make the proper right turn. Surely, you can point me in the right direction?"

"Oh, the tree that burned last spring is just past the old sunflower field."

"Past sunflowers. Okay, I can find that. Giant yellow flowers."

"Sure, yeah, except there ain't been no flowers bloom in a few years now."

"So it's a sunflower field without sunflowers?"

"Yeah, I reckon it is."

"Well, how am I supposed to find that?"

After selecting a jar of apple juice, I decide to take pity on the poor man. He's dressed to the nines in suit and tie and could possibly be here as an investor for the Ranch. Of course, if that were the case, he probably wouldn't have called the ranch a barn, but either way, my curiosity is piqued.

"Hey, Harry, I got gas on two."

"Sure thing. I got you all rang up here. Did you want me to put that on a charge account for you?"

"Not today. Thank you, though."

I turn to the bewildered man. "You're looking for Katherine? I think she's headed to the grocery."

"Yes! Well, no, I'm looking for her house. I was told Miss Smith was there today."

"Blakelynn Smith?" I ask.

"Yes. Have you seen her?"

"Well, yeah. Actually, I have."

"Was she with Mrs. Katherine?"

"She was, but she left."

"Do you know where she is headed now?"

171

"Well, I guess she's headed back to the ranch," I say and then hold out my hand. "Pleasure to meet you, Mr. . . . ?"

"Gooden. Mark Gooden. And you are?"

"Blakelynn Smith. Nice to meet you."

"You are Miss Blakelynn Smith?"

"I am."

He pulls out a manila envelope from the inside pocket of his suit jacket. "Miss Smith, you have been served," he says, passing the envelope to me. I stare at it dumbfounded while Mr. Gooden makes a hasty exit.

This is what I get for making fun of the poor man. Karma is a real bitch.

"Well, that wasn't nice, was it, Harry?"

"Should have let him search a little longer."

"Oh, well. Live and you learn. See you next time, Harry."

"Be safe, Miss Blake."

I toss the envelope on the seat when I crawl back in the truck and ignore it until I pull back up at Beau's. Then, sitting in the front yard, I peel back the top and pour the papers out, my pulse rate rising with each word I read.

That lowdown good for nothing piece of shit.

I climb from the truck and slam the door behind me. Beau is sitting at the kitchen table when I walk inside.

"Bad visit?"

I toss the papers on the table in front of him.

"Brad is suing me for half of Fresh Start."

"The hell you say."

"Yep," I say, slumping into one of the chairs across from him. "Claims he helped build it from the ground up."

"He didn't."

"I know."

I can't believe the nerve of him. I built this company from nothing while he pretended to love and care for me, and now he has the audacity to try to take it from me? With startling clarity, I see now why he came into town and why he was fine with my traveling and working so hard, even if it meant I had no time left for him. He never cared for me. He was in it for a paycheck. It made me wonder how long he'd been screwing Cindy. Was she part of all this? Only using me for what I was able to give them? The thought left a sour taste in my mouth.

"He won't get away with this, Blake."

"Oh, I know that. I'll make sure he regrets the day he ever met me." Pulling my cell from my back pocket, I click on the Southwest app and book a ticket back to Arizona, and then I send Shelly a text and ask if she can pick me up from the airport. I can Uber if I need to, but there are some other things I'd like to discuss with her if she's available.

"Give me a ride to the airport?" I ask Beau, and when he nods, I stand and head upstairs to pack a light bag. I don't know if I'll be able to get in to see the lawyer this late on a Friday, but I email anyway, requesting the earliest appointment.

"Brad Griffin isn't going to know what hit him."

CHAPTER TWENTY SEVEN

#myassissore

Calvin

DRIVING fifteen hours pulling a horse trailer isn't as easy as it used to be. Sometime over the last ten years, I'd gotten old. My ass hurts from sitting all day and my leg keeps cramping. A month ago, when Samantha called and asked if I would transport Billie to their new home, I agreed without a thought. Then Blake showed up and my life was once again turned upside down. I hadn't expected to get along with her at all. I damn sure didn't anticipate falling back in love with her, but if I was being honest, I had never fallen out. I'd pretended to be over her. I shut out all thought and memory of her. At least until nightfall, when she would creep into my dreams and haunt me until daybreak.

The most exquisite torture. In my dreams, she was still

mine. She loved me as much as I loved her, and we were happy. Some nights, she was round with my babe, while others, she was the laughing and carefree wild child of our youth. Every night, she was mine. When morning came, so did the reality that she was gone. And with the new light of day came the pain.

I had lived with it for so long I was no longer sure if I knew how to be happy. Every morning for the last month, I have woken and swallowed the misery, and then the sleep from my eyes would fade and I would remember she was back. She was here, and I had touched her, felt her, loved her.

It put the pep back in my step. I looked forward to showing up at the ranch every morning, and not just because I needed to keep my hands busy so my mind wouldn't dwell. She was there every day, greeting me with that smartass petal-soft mouth.

I called Samantha to cancel twice and backed out. I wasn't an oath breaker. I had given her my word and I would deliver.

I'm not sure what hurt worse, leaving Blake asleep in my bed at four AM or my ass after driving for fifteen hours. I don't even want to think about the fifteen headed home. At least Blake will be there to rub my sore muscles.

I pull the trailer around the circle drive and crawl from the cab of the truck. I stopped a few times to check on Billie's hay and water. Sometimes, they can get knocked over when a horse shifts or the trailer hits a rough patch in the road, but his was fine every time I stopped. I open the back gate and step in beside him, calling out his name and letting him know I'm there. I don't know if he understands a word I'm saying, but the sound of a voice lets them know someone is behind them. There's nothing quite as bad as a kick from a startled two-thousand-pound horse.

"Hey, you made it," Samantha says, walking around the back of the trailer. I back Billie up by tugging on the lead line. The trailer shakes and wobbles as he steps off.

"Yep. Where you want him?" I ask. I'm not trying to be rude, but now that I'm here, all I want to do is drop the trailer and hit the road.

"Let's put him in the new pasture. We finally got the fence finished last week."

I lead Billie over to the pasture gate and wait while Samantha swings open the gate. Billie was sick of riding too. He hops and bucks when I let him off the lead, stretching his legs and checking out the new place.

"Thanks for bringing him. I've got you a check inside for the transport and this last month's board. I'll be right back."

I nod and head back to the truck so I can start unhitching the trailer.

It's a quick process. I'm almost finished when Samantha pops back up. "Here ya go."

"Thanks. I'm gonna drop this here and hit the road, if that's all you need."

"Yep. That'll do it."

"If you need anything in the future, you've got my number."

"Have a safe trip back."

I tell her thank you again and finish dropping the trailer. I'm pulling my truck out from under the hitch when my cell rings. Blake's face pops up on the screen and I smile. I've only been gone a day and yet she already misses me.

"Hey, sexy, what are you doing?"

Her sinful laugh echoes across the line. "Headed to the airport."

"The airport?" I ask, my heart plummeting. The thought has always lodged in the back of my mind. *She's going to leave again.* It would creep out on occasion and harass me, but I didn't think she would be leaving this soon and without a goodbye.

"I've got some stuff to handle with the lawyers. I'm about to pull up, but I'll call you as soon as I land and fill you in."

"Okay, be safe."

"Thanks, you too."

I'd be lying if I said I hadn't hoped she would stay for good, even knowing the chances of that happening were slim to none. Blake had made a big life for herself on the West Coast. A life she has always dreamed of having. I'm proud of her. I just wish she had room in it for me too.

It's already late on the West Coast. Late on a Friday evening. The chances of her meeting with a lawyer today are nonexistent, which means she will be there all weekend, at least. I debate my options, walking a path in the dirt outside of my truck door. I should wait for her to call. I should trust her to not crush me again, but my chest is tight and my nerves frayed. I didn't want to lose her again. I can't.

Grabbing my cell off the seat of the truck where I tossed it, I text Beau.

Blake's gone to the airport.

I know. Just dropped her off. His reply is instant.

Well, fuck me. For a split second, the sting of betrayal takes my breath. My phone starts vibrating in my hand before I have a chance to text him back.

"Yeah?" I answer, anger flooding my tone.

"Figured you were probably losing your shit right about now." The sound of horns honking echoes through the phone. I calculate the time difference in my head. Rush hour in Birmingham is no joke. I try to avoid the whole area at all costs, but especially during rush hour traffic.

"You could say that."

"She will be back home on Tuesday. She booked a round-trip flight."

"She can change it." I hope she doesn't. The knowledge that she plans to return offers a little relief, but my chest is still tight.

"Yeah, but she won't. Don't worry."

"That's easy for you to say. She didn't leave you high and dry once already."

"Yeah, she did. She didn't just leave you, Cal. She left us all, and she came back. I trust her, and you should too."

I can tell he's worried too. He doesn't want me to know it, but when you've been friends for as long as we have, it's easy to read behind the words.

"Yeah. What the hell did she need to fly back out there for, anyway?"

"Her asshole ex is trying to sue her for rights to her company."

"The fuck?"

"Don't worry, she's got it handled."

I want to hop on the first plane and fly to her. I need to be by her side, but I know how that will look to her. She needs to know I trust her, even if I still struggle with the fear of losing her. I know that whatever decision she makes won't be done with malice. She not that type of person.

"Tell me everything."

Over the next twenty minutes, Beau fills me in on everything that has happened since I left yesterday morning. My temper rises with each passing second. If I ever get my hands on that weaseling son of a bitch, I'm liable to kill him. How the hell does he justify this shit in his head? There is no way in hell I'd be able to live off my woman for three years, and I damn sure wouldn't try to take the thing she built from the ground up, the thing she'd poured her blood, sweat, and tears into.

Piece of shit. That's not a man. That's scum.

The more I hear, the more I want to fly to Arizona. And not just to be there for Blake.

"I should go—"

"No. She's got this handled. She doesn't need either of us fighting her battles for her."

"But—"

He cuts me off again. He's right. But that doesn't mean I have to like it. "Calvin. She's got it."

CHAPTER TWENTY EIGHT

#fuckingex

Blake

MY FLIGHT back to Arizona lasts about four hours. The sun is starting to set across the Alabama horizon. When we land, the sky is tinged with the last vestiges of sunlight. I've always loved Arizona sunsets across the desert. The light reflects off the sandy dirt, creating a picture-perfect moment.

Shelly picks me up at the airport. I don't have any bags with me other than my carryon, so we head straight to the parking deck and her car. I fill her in on the papers I was served on the way to my house. I've read over them at least fifty times since the weasel had me served.

The thought that he believes I owe him any of my company blows my mind. He hasn't lifted one finger in the four years since I've known him. Four years I worked my ass off trying to make something of Fresh Start, a company I started on my own six years ago.

The lawyer's secretary penciled me in for Monday morning at eight. That leaves me with just over forty-eight hours to handle everything else I've been putting off here.

"Do you still have the information for the real estate agent who sold me the house?" I ask Shelly.

"Yeah. I have her stored in my phone. I planned on using her when I decide to sell my condo. Why? Are you planning to sell the house?"

"I guess so."

"Oh, man, are you sure? That place is worth what, $300k more now than when you bought it? It's a great location and prime residential, great schools. It's like a five out of five."

"I don't need it. I could keep it, but I'm not planning to live in Arizona anymore."

Shelly gawks in my direction wide-eyed until traffic forces her to put her eyes back on the road.

"I'm sorry. I know I just sprang that on you. I planned to talk to you about it this weekend. How about we stop at Durant's and talk over dinner?" I ask, knowing she won't turn down a chance to eat at the city's best fine dining establishment. After my in-flight peanuts and Coke, I could stand to put something more substantial in my stomach.

"Sure." She clicks on the blinker to change lanes so she can exit I-10.

I had planned to approach the subject with more grace than I did. Shelly is a wonderful assistant. Truthfully, the title *Assistant* does her little justice. She's my left hand, right hand, and frontal lobe all rolled into a perky, charming, sophisticated package. I'm so thankful she found me all those years ago and demanded that I accept her help.

When I first began taking the idea of starting a company for myself seriously, I hit the ground running. I wasn't the type of chick who could sit and weigh options. I decided in a second and then dealt with the fallout. I've never been one to jump between this or that. So, in typical Blake fashion, when the thought struck, I jumped.

And then fell.

Hard.

I had no idea what it meant to run my own company or to be my own boss. I lacked the structure needed to make it work. My mind flited between ideas like a hummingbird between flowers. I had no direction and a shit ton of ambition.

I was flailing, drowning, ready to quit it all when Shelly messaged me. She had read a blog post, loved it, and wanted more. I didn't have more at the time. I had gotten distracted with something else and hadn't updated my website in months. She offered to help.

I paid her in hugs and funny memes.

Then the blog took off and I started the podcast. I went from eating ramen to dining on the best of the best. Shelly had stuck by me through it all. She was more than an assistant to me. She was my lifesaver.

"So, you're leaving Arizona." It's not a question. She knows me better than I know myself, and once my mind is made up, it's done.

"Yes." I take a sip of my wine and wait for her to process that.

"Because of Brad?" she asks.

"No. Not at all. Actually, Brad is the only reason I thought about staying. I hate the idea of his thinking he chased me out of town." It still left a bad taste in my mouth.

"Then why?" she asks, and I don't get angry or frustrated with the question. I understand why she's confused. For years, I've talked about Alabama with nothing but disdain. Until going back, that is how I remembered it.

"It's home. I know I've always said I hated it, but now that I'm there? I can't imagine being anywhere else," I tell her truthfully.

"I understand." And that's the thing about Shelly. She's genuinely happy for me. Even if finding my happiness means a lot of unknowns for her. I can almost physically see her mind working, planning for the future.

"Relocating Fresh Start to Alabama shouldn't be that hard. It's mostly online, anyway."

"Well, that's what I wanted to talk to you about. I don't want to move Fresh Start. I want you to take it over." I hold my breath and wait. I hope this is something Shelly would want, but it's hard to gauge. She's never complained about her job, so I don't know if the idea of having more will appeal to her or not.

"What?"

"I want to assign you as CEO or President of Fresh Start. I will still own the company, but as CEO, I'll sign over ten percent of all shares to you."

"You're serious?"

"Yes. You've worked your ass off for this company, and you're the only person I could ever trust to take over. This is your baby, too."

She leans back in her chair and stares. "You're serious?" she asks again.

"Yes. I'm positively serious. I'll have the lawyers draw up the paperwork Monday."

"Holy fu . . ." I laugh into my napkin. That's the closest I've heard Shelly come to cursing.

"I'm assuming this comes with a raise?" she asks.

"A big one."

"Nice. In that case, can I buy your house?"

"Hell, yeah." That settled, we move on to more important things. Food. By the time my plate arrives, I feel like I could eat an entire cow. Not that I would, but I'm starving so I can't really be trusted. My phone dings halfway through the meal, and I pull it from my purse. Fireflies take off in my belly when I read the text from Calvin. It's a picture of the Alabama night sky. The ranch is far enough from the city that none of the city lights affect the view of stars.

Almost as beautiful as you.

I smile and reply with a picture of my half-eaten steak.

Almost as tasty as you.

"Okay, chick. Dish."

"Huh?" I ask, putting away my phone.

"I know that face. You've been holding out on me. I want details."

I spend the rest of the meal with a grin on my face that I can't seem to wipe off. I tell her all about Calvin from years ago and then catch her up on Calvin from right now. I've become a blubbering girl who only wants to talk about her boyfriend. Shelly doesn't seem to mind. It's been a while since we sat and talked about nothing. It's nice. By the time we finish dinner and she drops me at the house, I've caught her up on everything and calmed her worrying heart.

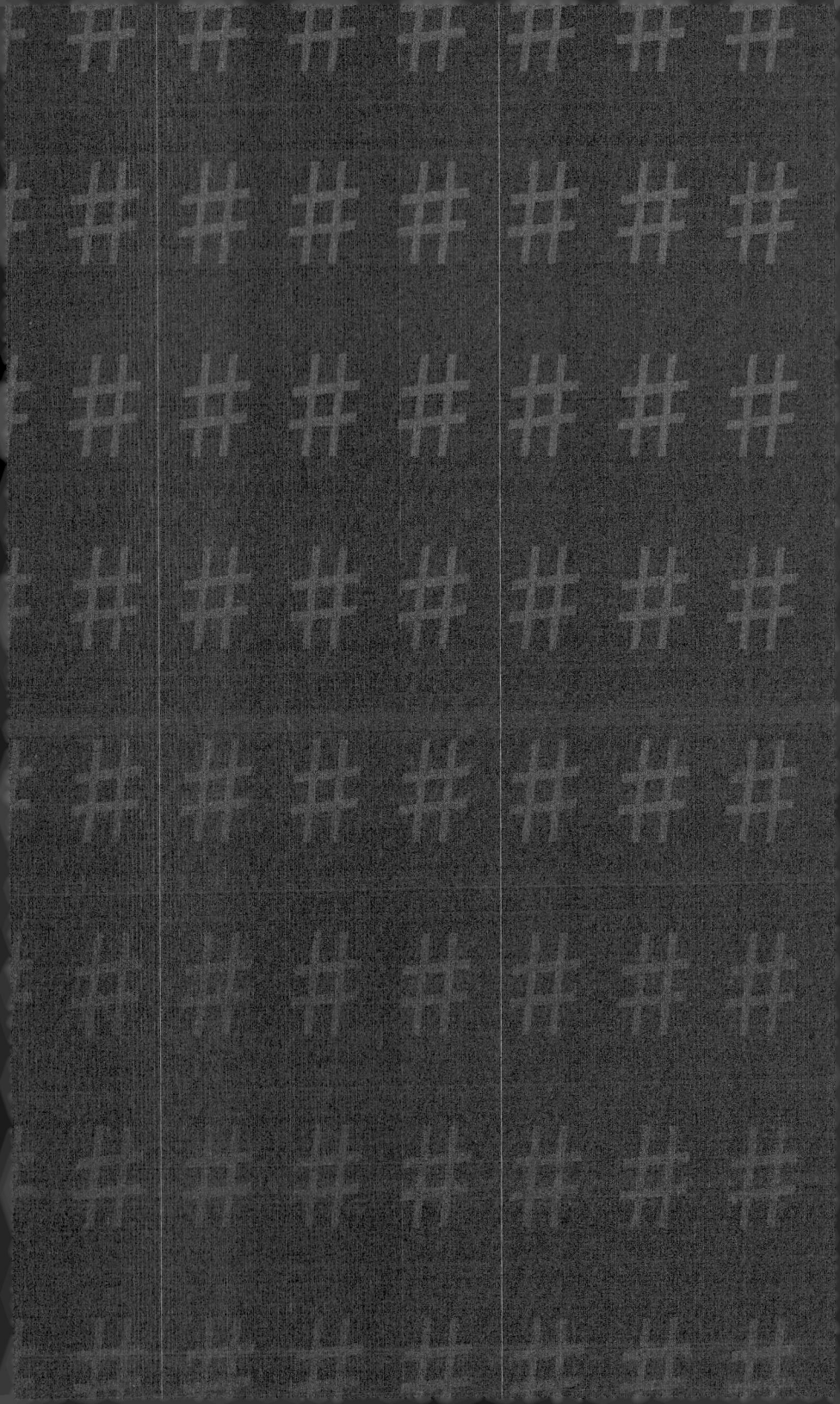

CHAPTER TWENTY NINE

#Tipsy

Calvin

BLAKE CALLS AS SOON as her friend drops her at her house. Her voice sounds a little high-pitched, and every couple of seconds, she giggles. I imagine her there all alone, stumbling through the house, flicking on lights, and peeling off layers of clothing.

It's killing me to not be there with her.

"What are you doing?" I stack the pillows on my bed against the hotel headboard and lean back. It's gotten late here, but with the time difference, it's barely ten PM there.

"About to take a shower if I can find a towel in this place." She grunts, mumbling to herself, "Ah, got one. Shit." Her voice disappears for a second, followed by more rustling. "I dropped you."

"That wasn't very nice."

"Oops. You'll be okay." I want to kiss the slight slur off her lips and then run my tongue along every inch of her body until she can't form another thought.

"Take your clothes off and start the shower."

"Wha...?"

"Don't argue. Just listen. Is there someplace you can set your phone so it doesn't get messed up?"

"Yeah. I think so."

"Good. Put me there and then answer my FaceTime." I tap the *Video Call* button on the screen. It's a pretty cool feature that I had no idea about until last week when Blake showed me. I plan to use it for all its worth tonight. Blake answers the call and then sets her phone down and stands back. She's already lost all of her clothes. Her skin begs to be touched.

She turns the dials on and steps back, waiting for the water to warm.

"What are you planning here?" she asks, stepping into the shower stall and leaving the door open so the phone won't fog up.

"Pour some shampoo into your palm and wash your hair. You're not going to want to fool with it in a few minutes." She does as instructed, and I watch her scrub the shampoo to bubbling suds before rinsing and adding conditioner. The sight of her glistening wet skin has my cock straining for attention in my jeans.

"Okay, now what?" Her hands wrap around her chest, trying to cover herself.

"Since your hair is clean, let's concentrate on more important things, like your body. Squirt some body wash into your hands."

She pours body wash into her empty hands. "Okay."

"Now spread the body wash in your hands over your soft, wet breasts. I love your fucking breasts."

I imagine taking one in my hand and rubbing the wash across her taut nipple. "Feel the water cascading over your shoulders and running down over the mounds of your breasts, streaming off your stiff nipples." She closes her eyes, tilting her head back. I know it's stupid, but I'm so fucking jealous of the spray of water right now. I'd give anything to be there with her, running my fingers feather-soft across the perky mounds. "Does that feel good?"

She nods her head. When she lifts her breasts, kneading them, my cock jumps in my pants. I've never seen a more glorious sight in my life than the one of her standing under a streaming waterfall, following my every command. The water washes away all traces of soap, leaving her skin squeaky clean and begging for my touch. She leans against the shower wall, and it might be my imagination, but I think her chest is rising and falling faster than it was a few minutes ago.

"Open up your hands and slide your nipples between your fingers. Caress and pinch them." She follows my direction without a moment's hesitation. Her hands trace along every curve and hollow with the care of an artist.

Her moan echoes in the shower stall, and my cock twitches in my jeans.

"I'm so fucking hard right now, Blake."

"Slip a hand down over your belly and between your legs and rub your clit with your fingers. Imagine me licking you, sucking your clit, making you pant."

I unzip my pants and my cock springs free. Seeing Blake masturbating in the shower with my words as her guide has done nothing for my sanity, but the sight has made me rock-hard. My hand grips the base of my cock, and I pull, tugging on it in long, slow, torturous strokes. I squeeze the head and twist my hand in semi-circle motions before sliding back down, spreading a trail of precum as I go.

"Shit, I'm not the best at this facetime thing, but I'm going to try to do it one-handed. The thought of you touching yourself in the shower, following my commands, getting off because of me . . . it's making me horny as hell. I'm stroking my cock watching you."

A whimper escapes her lips. "I want to see. Show me," she demands.

I prop my phone up on the nightstand and angle it so she can watch me stroke myself.

"Slide two fingers inside yourself. Feel how soft that sweet pussy is."

She moves the phone to a bench in the corner and then sits across the stall under the spray of water. I can see every fucking beautiful inch of her body.

"I want you to slide your fingers out and circle around your clit, tease yourself with your wet juices." I stroke up and down faster and faster while she does the same. I'm so fucking close to exploding, but I hold off so I can make sure she finishes first.

"Now go back into your slick wet pussy and pump your fingers in and out. Rub your palm against your clit as you stroke inside." She's panting, her body quivering with the anticipation of release. "Fucking hell, Blake. I'm about to come for you. Are you ready? Can you come for me, baby?"

She nods, barely, curling her fingers inside herself and then sliding out, circling once, twice, and sliding back inside. Her free hand reaches for her breast, and sliding her nipple between her finger and thumb, she pinches, tugs, while the other hand slaps against her clit, her fingers pounding into her glistening pussy.

My body twitches. I grind out her name and tilt my head back against the headboard, gasping while the waves of my orgasm wash through me again and again until a warm calm takes its place. Blake is slouched against the wall, staring at the ceiling of the shower stall, trying to right her breathing. But that sinful grin tells me everything I need to know.

"Fuck, Blake. You drive me wild."

She laughs and stands on wobbly legs to rinse off before shutting off the shower and wrapping herself in a fluffy white towel.

"I can be out there by eight tomorrow morning if you give me the word." I mean it. The only keeping me here, 1500 miles from her, is her. If she says the word, I will book the ticket right now and fly out of here.

"No. I'm fine here, and I'll be home before you know it."

My heart stops when I hear those words. I haven't heard her refer to Alabama as home in a long time, if ever. The fact that she sees it that way now has me wanting to shout from the rooftop. The raging desire to chase her down has consumed me since she called and told me she was heading to the airport. Talking to Beau helped a little, but not as much as hearing it from her own lips.

"If you're sure, but I perform better in person." That gains a laugh from her.

"Where are you? That doesn't look like your room." Pulling back the comforter, she crawls into bed and turns on her side.

"I stopped for the night in Winchester," I said.

"Oh, okay. Room looks nice."

"It would be nicer if you were in the bed next to me and not two thousand miles away." I hope to pull another smile from her, but the comment seems to sober her.

"I meant to catch you up on all the stuff here, but I got distracted with Shelly and then the shower."

"It's okay, Beau filled me in. If you need me for anything, I'm a call away."

"I know. And thank you, but I really am okay. I meet with the lawyer on Monday, and I'm sure he will straighten it all out."

"What do you have planned this weekend? Catching up with friends?"

"Yeah, I guess. I've got a few other things to handle while I'm here. I've been putting them off, but now is as good a time as any." She stretches, yawning.

"Get some sleep, beautiful."

"Okay. Text me in the morning before you head out?"

"Sure. 'Night."

"'Night."

She hangs up the phone and I miss her immediately. I almost call her back just to tell her that, but I know she's tired and needs rest so I plug my phone into the charger and roll over, pulling the comforter over my head. I'm out within minutes.

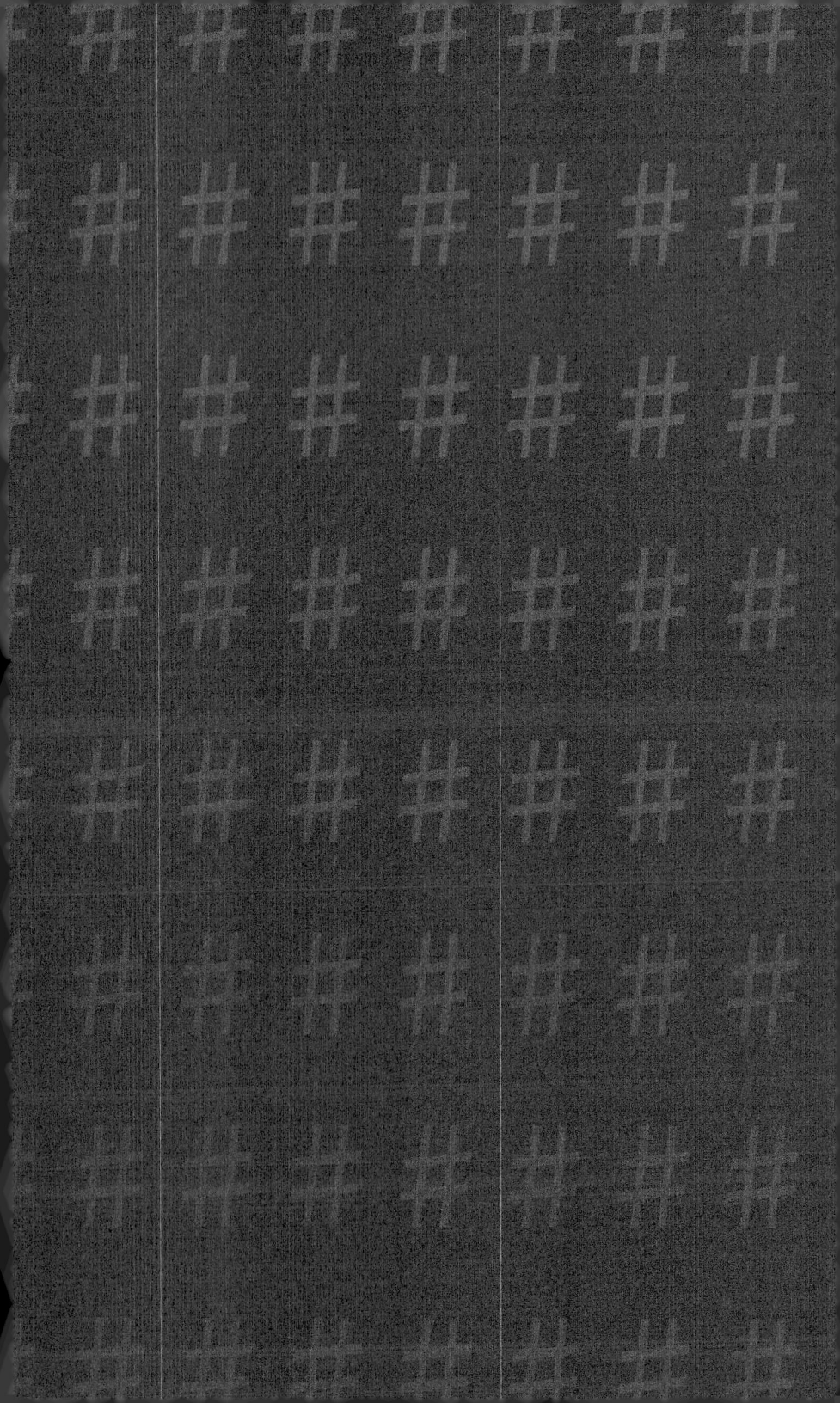

CHAPTER THIRTY

#movingon

Blake

MY FINAL PASS-THROUGH of the house is bittersweet. I never wanted this place. It's too big for only two people and so much space went wasted, but after a while, it grew on me. The plan had been to remain here for the next ten to fifteen years. To build my life around this home.

Plans change. And sometimes, those changes borrow your favorite dress and sleep with your fiancé. I'm still bitter, but not over the loss of Brad. For five years, Cindy was my closest friend other than Shelly. The house holds so many memories of us together, celebrating our respective big wins, crying over our losses, and pushing each other harder, farther than we ever thought we'd go.

I miss that Cindy. Not the lying bitch who screwed Brad behind my back.

After meeting with the real estate agent Saturday, I'm ready to close this chapter of my life. She had taken the extra key I'd made when she left that afternoon. Shelly is already talking to her about buying, but the house will need to be appraised and then listed before she can move closer to the buying phase. Personally, I just want it over. The sooner, the better.

My phone dings, alerting me. The Uber driver I scheduled has arrived. I set my spare key on the counter and close the front door behind me with a final click. When we close, I'll need to come back, but otherwise, I'm done. Any and all correspondence will now go through the agent.

It's a quarter after seven when I climb in the backseat, forty-five minutes before I need to be at the lawyer's office, and the city is already bustling with morning commuters.

Headed in now.

Calvin's response is immediate.

Good luck.

I don't believe in luck. I believe in hard work and dedication, but I don't text him that back. Instead, I send a kiss face emoji and turn my phone on silent, then I step through the glass double doors and take the elevator up to the ninth floor.

"Miss Smith. I'll let Mr. Howard know you're here. Would you like a bottle of water or some coffee while you wait?"

"No, thank you."

The office is large, expanding across the entire floor, but the décor offers a modernized, cozy sense. Stark white walls are softened with warm, colorful tapestries. I sit in a butter-soft leather chair and wait to be called. It doesn't take long.

"Blakelynn, so good to see you again." Doug Howard has been a godsend over the last few years. When I first started Fresh Start, I didn't put any thought into the legalities of the business. All I wanted to do was share myself with the world and build a life out of it. Doug dropped into my lap like an angel sent from heaven one day, and I haven't let him go. He was married to one of Shelly's cousins at the time, although I believe they have since divorced. We were throwing a surprise birthday party for Shelly, and he'd popped by for a few minutes. We started talking, and his few minutes turned to hours. By the end of the night, I had secured him as my counsel, and I don't regret the decision a bit.

"How are you, Doug?" Leaning forward, I kiss the air on the side of his face while he squeezes me into a formal hug.

"I've been good, really good. Now tell me what we have going on." We take a few steps down the hall and turn into his office. He lifts his hand, waving to the empty seat across from his desk. It takes less than ten minutes for me to catch him up on the breakup and what followed, including Brad showing up in Alabama. Doug doesn't look surprised in the least. He's never been a fan of Brad.

"Well, let's start with congratulations. It's about time you saw that scum for what he is and kicked him to the curb. For the life of me, I can't figure out how or why you allowed him to live off you for the last three years, anyway."

"I don't guess I paid attention. He wasn't bothering me, and honestly, I thought I was lucky he wasn't being an ass about all the time I spent away, or my forgetfulness and distracted mind."

"He didn't complain because he enjoyed it. He had the best

setup. A woman who didn't care what money he spent, and she was gone, leaving him to do as he pleased."

"I know that now. I've been stupid."

"No, just trusting. It's done. I'll need copies of your credit card statements and bank account for the last three years. I want to highlight all expenses you didn't use. As far as the case, I don't see a reason we can't have it thrown out. I'll work on it and call you if I need anything else."

"Okay. Thank you, Doug."

"Don't worry. This is why I'm here. We have contracts and stipulations in place to cover this. He can't touch the company. Now, tell me what we want to do with Shelly."

"She's deserved this for a long time. I've just been too busy and didn't slow down enough to make the change."

"Well, you know I think Shelly hung the moon, so of course she deserves it. But we need to work out what the new position means, how much control over the company she has, what percentage you're offering her, and her salary, to name a few things."

We go back and forth, discussing the new position until my stomach growls, shocking us both. "Is it that time already?" The clock on the wall ticks closer and closer to noon. We've been talking for hours and I hadn't even noticed. "Would you like to join me for lunch?" Doug asks, standing.

"That sounds nice. Let me freshen up and I'll meet you in the lobby."

I text Cal from the ladies' powder room and let him know how things are going. It's been hard on him, staying back home while I'm here dealing with a psycho ex, but so far, we're making it work. It's strange to miss him. Every free moment I get, I find myself reaching for my phone to update him or just

THE WAY WE LOVED

check in. Before, with Brad, I could go days without talking to him and then when he would call, and I would get irritated that I had to take time away from what I'd been working on to speak to him. The differences are staggering and eye opening. It's not the first time I've asked myself why the hell I stayed with Brad as long as I did. I still didn't have an answer.

I miss you.

My heart flutters when I read those words, and the grin that stretches across my face couldn't be torn off with the force of a thousand pounds' pressure. He lights something within me that has been extinguished for so long I'd forgotten it was there. For years, I've been dulling myself down for others while standing in front of thousands and thousands of people, telling them not to. My motto in life was to live your truth regardless of whether others understood or approved, and this whole time, I've been living a lie.

Somewhere along the way, I started fighting for others and stopped fighting for myself. No more. From this day forward, I want to do what brings me joy, what lights me from the inside out, and what puts a smile on my face that no force can erase, and I'm not talking about a man, either. Although he is a part of what fills me with joy right now, but what I'm talking about goes so much deeper than a relationship with another person.

When I wake in the morning, it is going to be to the sound of music I want to hear. When I lay my head in the bed at night, it's going to be in the home I want. The place I chose for me, surrounded by items collected by me, for me. No more of this breaking for others. I can bend, but I will never again break for another person.

Doug is waiting at the exit when I enter the lobby. Together, we walk the two blocks to the restaurant with my stomach singing the marching anthem. When I was first served, a dozen emotions coursed through me at once. I was pissed and upset, and that damn sense of betrayal crept back in, but now all I feel is thankful. Brad might not know it, but he helped me a lot by forcing me back here. I closed a lot of doors, doors that had been swinging wildly in the breeze, and now I can officially give myself the fresh start I've worked so hard to give others.

CHAPTER THIRTY ONE

#flipthatshed

Calvin

"WHERE DO YOU WANT THIS?" I step off the ladder and turn to find Beau standing a few feet away, a bundle of two by fours balanced on his shoulder and my mother by his side.

"Toss the boards over there and give this one to me," I say, pulling my mother in for a quick, sweaty hug. Beau takes off in the direction of the house, Neo trailing behind him. "Bring me one, too." If the man is going to drink all my beer, the least he could do is deliver me one.

For the last three days, I've spent every daylight hour since coming back from Pennsylvania working on a surprise for Blake. Hearing her call Alabama home did something to me. Up until that moment, I believed I would lose her again, but now, I'm determined to make sure I don't.

Since our official coming out at the bar, Blake has spent more nights at my place than the studio above Beau's, and even though I know we aren't ready to move in—well, she's not ready—I still want her to have her own space here. "I like what you've done with the place." I know sarcasm when I hear it, and Mom is the queen of sarcasm.

"It's going to be nice when I'm finished." Glancing around, I can already see the finished product. Thirty-six hours ago, this was nothing but a shed to store Christmas decorations in.

"Define nice," she says.

"Do you think she'll like it?" I hope she does. I wanted to do something for her, give her something that I know she will use.

"Who? Blake?"

"Yes, Mother. Who else?"

"Well, then, I think that depends on what it is and what you're trying to accomplish."

"Blake likes taking photos, and she needs space she can work in if she wants to. I don't want to accomplish anything. I just want her to have a space that is hers."

"Hers. Is that why you're refinishing a building on your property?"

"What the hell, Mom? I don't care about that. She can move it to her own land if she wants. I just wanted to make her feel at home."

"I see."

"What's that mean? Do you not approve?"

"Oh, Son, of course I approve. I've always wanted Blake for you. I just wanted to make sure your head and your heart were in the right place before I gave you this," She says, pulling a black box from her pocket. I've seen it a hundred times sitting on the armoire in her bedroom over the years and may have taken a peek once or twice. My hands shake a little as I peel back the lid. "It was Blake's great-grandmother's, passed down through the generations. Her mama trusted me to give it to you. You were always her pick for Blake too.

"I want you to have it now. You can have the stone reset if you think Blake would like something more modern, but when the time is right, I'd love for you to ask her with this."

"Thank you. She will love it just the way it is. I can't believe Tricia planned this too."

"She planned a lot. That's all she could do toward the end. I wish she were still here. She'd be so proud of Blake and all she has done."

"I like to think she still is."

"You're right. She is."

I pull her in for a hug, kissing the top of her head, and I don't let her go until the tears burning behind my lids fade.

"You gonna stick around and help out?" I tuck the ring into my pants where it sits burning a hole in my pocket.

"Not a chance, but call me when you're ready to decorate or shop and I'll stop back by." Figures, but what did I expect? I've never met a woman who wanted to get nasty tearing something apart.

I've almost finished the second phase of the project. The first phase was tearing everything out and cleaning up the mess. Since then, I've framed in the rooms and added open lighting to the room facing the eastern sun so she'll have plenty of natural light if she wants it, and if not, she can go in the back room that I've made into a darkroom.

When I first started, I had no clue what to do with any of it, but Janie was able to pull up some photos on a website called pin something or another and then order plans once I decided on the path I wanted to take. Plans I could understand, could read and work with. The rest of that shit was out of my league of expertise.

"Actually, since you volunteered, can you grab Janie and make a Home Depot run for me? She has the pictures of what I need. Everything else is up to y'all."

"Sure, Son." Reaching into my back pocket, I pull out my billfold and pass her my credit card. There's a split second when she reaches for it that I ask myself whether it's a good idea to let a woman loose with unlimited funds in Home Depot, but I shrug it off. What's the worst they can do?

I find out three hours later.

How the hell they managed to buy this much shit in such a short time frame I will never know. Beau finished nailing up the sheetrock and plastering the mud on it while I installed the windows. We have to let the mud sit and dry before sanding it down and painting, but now that the women are back, I'll be able to start the floors. The goal was to have the place done before Blake comes home. It's going to be close, but I think we'll make it. If not, I'll have to make up an excuse for her not coming over to my place until I finish.

Speak of the devil. My phone flashes with a text from Blake.

Finishing up here. Things are good. He's gonna handle it. He said Brad doesn't have a leg to stand on, so I feel better except I'm starving, lol.

Good. I figured he would take of you. Go eat.

I'm about to. We're walking over to a cute Italian place. I'll call you when I leave.

Knowing her lawyer has her back is a relief. I didn't think jackass Brad would get anything from her, but I don't know how all that works in the legal world. It's terrifying to think that in that aspect, I can't protect her, no matter how much I want to. At the end of the day, all I want is for Blakelynn to feel safe and loved, and I want the hollow, empty look that burned like a shadow in her eyes when she first arrived to never reappear, even if she isn't able to find those things with me.

 I glance at the she shed that is about three-quarters of the way done and at the group of people who have shown up every morning at the crack of dawn the last three days to make it happen, and then I text her back and tell her I miss her because I don't ever want her to wonder about my heart and whether she is the most important thing in the world to me. I want—no, I need—her to know she is it.

CHAPTER THIRTY TWO

#headinghome

Blake

MY FLIGHT out of Arizona was delayed an hour, and by the time I make it to Birmingham, I'm ready to drink a glass—bottle—of wine and soak in a hot bath, and it's only eleven AM.

A blue Ford pulls up to the curbside pickup. With the window rolled down, I hear Beau call for me to get in. "Where's Cal?" I ask, slamming the passenger door closed.

"What? No 'I miss you, Beau. Thank you for picking me up. It's great to see you.'"

"Sorry. Long morning and my head is killing me."

"There's some Advil in the glove compartment."

After digging for a few minutes, I locate the bottle and take three, knocking them back with a sip of my apple juice, and then I lean back in the seat and pull my sunglasses over my eyes.

We're almost home before the pain subsides and I appear human again. Beau has remained quiet the whole drive, listening to the country music station on his Sirius radio and ignoring me.

"How the hell did you get roped into picking me up?" he never answered my question earlier, and at the time, my head hurt too much to think about it.

"Cal got tied up and asked me to come. No biggie. I didn't have anything planned for the day. How was the trip?"

"Good. Better than I expected, to be honest. I sold my house."

"You did what? How?"

"I mean, it isn't sold yet, but I put it on the market, and I have a potential buyer already lined up, so I guess that means you're stuck with me for a little longer until I can find my own place down here."

"What about your mom's place?"

"I guess I could go there if you're ready for your place back. I haven't been by there in years. The place is probably a dump."

"No, you can stay as long as you want. I don't mind, but if you decide to check out your mom's, I think you will be surprised to find it weathering just fine."

"Really?"

"Blake. There was no way in hell Cal was going to let that place fall to the wayside just because you left. He knew what it meant to you and your mom. He's kept it up."

"All these years?"

"Yep. It's empty, but the power and water are on and the place is clean."

THE WAY WE LOVED

There are no words in the English language to describe the way that makes me feel. My chest tightens and my eyes burn with the tears clogging my throat. The fact that he did that, not knowing when or if he would ever see me again, shows the type of man Calvin Hunt is. Nobility, honesty, respectfulness, kindness, and generosity are only a few of his attributes. And then I realize he never intended to tell me because that's not who is. He doesn't do something for the recognition he will receive. He does it because that's what's right, and his heart won't allow him to do wrong. He is a good man, one of the last few good ones out there.

"Can we stop by there?" Tears stream down my cheeks, but I'm not sad. Overwhelmed, maybe. Astonished, for sure, but not sad.

Beau doesn't answer, but when we come to the fork, instead of going right and taking me to his place, he turns left. I hold my breath when he turns into the drive and as we pass the rows of weeping willows. It's not until the front porch comes into view that I release it. I'm not sure what I expected, but the perfectly manicured yard and fresh paint on the doors and shutters wasn't it.

Beau stops the truck at the end of the drive and waits next to me until I gain enough courage to step out of the truck. We walk side by side up the steps I sat on as a child, coloring or playing pretend with my Barbie and Ken, past the rocker my mother drank her coffee from every morning, to the front door. I lift the pot next to the door and find a spare key, the same place my mom left it. When I push it into the door, it turns with the ease of a well-lubricated lock. The door swings open, and I'm flooded by memories of my childhood home. It smells of cedar and honeysuckles and a hint of lemon, the same kind you would smell in a can of furniture polish. I step through the door, beau by my side, and turn on lights as I make my way through the house.

Calvin hasn't touched or moved anything. It looks exactly the same as it did the day I left, but it's clean, just the way Beau said it would be. I stop in the hall and look at all the pictures hung there, pictures dating back to a time before I knew what cancer was and that I should be afraid. Back to a time when the only thing I cared about was the pink ribbon at the end of my braids. At the end of the long hall is a closed door that leads to my mother's room. I twist the knob and push the door open and then close it back behind me. For eleven years, I have been running from memories of her, both good and bad, because they hurt equally.

I've quit running now.

When I sit on the blue and red quilt laying across her bed, I can almost imagine her there next to me, singing softly in the background or twisting the hair out of my face and tucking it behind my ear the way she always did. She's gone and she's never coming back, but I've been doing her a disservice by trying to pretend she never existed. It may have hurt less at the time, but I also lost a piece of who I am at my very core. Tricia Smith raised me to be a strong, independent woman, to care for others and never turn my back on a friend. She made me the person I am today, and I walked away from her.

I vow from that moment forward not to push the thought or memory of her away ever again. I will endure the sting of pain and rejoice in the joyful bliss. When I step out of the room, I take a detour to the bathroom and splash cool water on my face before finding Beau again.

"I can't believe he did this."

"Can't you though? It's Cal. He knew you would need this one day. Neither of us knew when, but it was bound to happen at some point. You can't run from the past forever, Buttercup."

I lean into his arms and soak in the warmth of his embrace. "I love you, asshole. Thank you for bringing me."

"Right back at ya, champ. Now, can we get home before Cal hunts me down for keeping you away?"

"Yeah, let's go."

I don't know what I will do with the house or all the belongings in it, but when I lock the door behind us, I know I'll be back, and this time, eleven years won't pass before I return. This place is as much a piece of me as my mother. The thought of ever losing it doesn't sit well, but at the same time, I don't know if I would be able to mentally handle living here every day. I make a mental note to check into possibly renting the place out after I finish going through all of our belongings. Maybe.

Calvin is waiting outside when we pull up with a blindfold and my camera. I'd be lying if I said my heart didn't leap at the sight of him. When the truck rolls to a stop I climb out and run to him, jumping into his arms. He stumbles back a few steps to keep from falling over.

"Thank you." My lips press to his. "Thank you, thank you, thank you." Every time I kiss him, I thank him again. It will never be enough, and I know that, but I want to show him how much I appreciate what he's done for me and my mother, even if she isn't here to thank him herself.

"We stopped by Tricia's" Beau says by way of explanation and Cal nods in understanding. When I feel I've covered his face in enough kisses, I wiggle and make him set me down.

"I should have told you already."

"It doesn't matter. It's perfect."

"Come on. I had a surprise planned for you."

"Another one? I don't know if my heart can handle anything else today."

"Trust me?" he asks and holds up the blindfold. Tingling sparks of excitement zing straight to the apex of my thighs. I've never been into the kinkier side of sex, but after today, I'm willing to do whatever he asks of me.

My face must give away my thoughts. "Not that, my little vixen. The blindfold is for the surprise."

"Perv," Beau calls, jumping back into his truck, and I blush. Of course, he wouldn't be offering that, especially not in front of Beau. What was I thinking?

"Maybe later," Cal whispers in my ear before sliding his arms behind my legs and sweeping me off my feet. "The surprise is at my house."

"Is it a pony? Oh, Daddy, I've always wanted a real pony!" My attempt to hide my embarrassment has always been to joke and use sarcasm, and this time is no different.

"Shut up." Cal drops me at the passenger side of his truck and then leaves me to climb in on my own.

"Humph. I guess chivalry really is dead."

"I heard that."

I stick out my tongue. "I meant for you to."

Before we pull into Calvin's drive, he stops the truck on the side of the road and makes me face toward the window so he can tie the blindfold around my eyes. I hate surprises. Like I really, really hate surprises. I never react the way it's expected, so I end up thinking about how I'm supposed to react so much that when the surprise is unveiled, I forget to react at all.

At least this time, I don't know days in advance, so I have

very little time to psych myself out of it. It's strange to feel the truck glide along the gravel drive and hear the crunch but not see it. It opens my senses to other things as well, for instance, the intoxicating scent of Cal. He smells of horses and wood shavings mixed with the light fragrance of his morning aftershave.

When he reaches out and touches me, I yelp and jump in my seat, not expecting it, and he laughs. "Sorry."

"It's okay. Just caught me by surprise. Get it? Ha-ha."

"I'm going to walk around and open your door, Miss Chivalry is Dead, unless you think you can make it across the yard on your own."

"Don't be a dick. Obviously, I want you to carry me the whole way. What kind of gal do you take me for?"

He doesn't reply, and before I know what's happening, my door is pulled open and he's tossed me over his shoulder.

"Calvin Hunt. I'm going to kick your ass for this. Put. Me. Down."

I hear the snicker of someone else, and my cheeks redden, knowing others are around to see him carry me like a sack of potatoes. I will pay him back for this.

"I'm going to take off the blindfold now. Are you ready?"

I nod my head, and he sets me back on my own two feet, turning my body in the direction he wants me to face, and then he pulls the covering from my eyes. I'm staring at a row of cars in the driveway and Cal, who is standing in front of me. He smiles and grabs my shoulders, spinning me around. My hand rises, covering the silent O on my lips.

It's beautiful.

"I wanted you to have a space just for you," he says, watching me and waiting for my reaction. His mom and Beau are standing to the side, waiting for me with smiles matching the one I know I should be making, but I can't.

I cant handle this man. He is too good to me. Or at least that's how it feels, but when you go through life only loving yourself a little, like say, twenty percent, when someone comes along and loves you a little more, you think you've won the lottery, but in fact, they aren't loving you right either.

It's not until you find the courage to love yourself at the fullest, one hundred percent, that you see you've been cheated, and then when someone comes along and loves you more, that is when you've reached the jackpot. Calvin loves me more. And he shows me that every single day.

I turn to him and pull him to me and bury my face in his chest. And then I break. The tears that come are months, years of suppressed pain and joy and longing all rolled into a sob that shakes the ground I'm standing on. He wraps his arms around me and smooths the hair down my back while murmuring nonsense in my ear. Nothing else exists outside of us, here and now. Not the building he transformed into a magical oasis, not our friends and family, not a single thing.

I cry for minutes, hours, seconds, until the bank of tears dries up and the well of overwhelming emotion passes. When I peel myself from his chest and look around, everyone else is gone. I almost feel bad, but I like the idea of seeing what they did without an audience.

"Show me?"

"Right this way, beautiful."

The first thing I notice is the floor to ceiling windowpanes that span the length of the eastern wall. My pulse skips a beat when I imagine the lighting coming in there first thing in the morning. I take my time exploring every nook and cranny.

When I stumble across something new, Cal explains his reasoning for it and what he hoped I would use it for, like the blacked-out room in the far back corner.

It's easily the most perfect present he could have ever given me. Slowly, the others creep back inside, and I hug each one of them and thank them for the amazing gift. It's been years since someone did anything for me just because and didn't expect something in return for it. In retrospect, I now want to do something equally inspiring for each of them. It's funny how the gift of giving ignites that passion in others.

CHAPTER THIRTY THREE

#stopthetears

Calvin

FUCKING HELL.

    When Blake broke down, I nearly lost it. It took everything in me to stand there and hold her while she unloaded her soul into my shirt. I hated the idea that she was in pain of any kind, much less the type of pain that would cause the shaking sobs that erupted from her. As soon as she started crying, I waved the others away, wanting to give her as much privacy as I could in that moment. It wasn't much, but it's all I had to offer.

    Seeing her smile now almost erases the memory of her clinging to me like a lifeline. Almost, but not quite. She moves through the building, taking in every detail with an artist's mind and with the joy of a child on Christmas morning. This is the reaction I had hoped for when I planned the surprise unveiling.

Beau steps closer to me, leaving Mom in the room with Blake. "She's been through hell, man."

"I know. It fucking kills me."

"Me too. But she's home now."

I choke my own tears back when he says that, not wanting to give her any reason to worry. Beau slaps me on the back, and the sting is the extra push I need to shove them back down.

"I'll take care of her."

"*We* will. She might be the love of your life, but she's like a sister to me."

"I know, and you're right. We will."

"I'm gonna head up to the house and light the grill. Did you marinate the meat?"

"Yeah, I put it in the fridge so Neo wouldn't take it off the counter. Mom brought a few sides, and some of her famous peach cobbler, too."

"Sweet baby Jesus. I can't promise that will be there when y'all make it up."

"It had better be, or Blake will be kicking your ass. You know how she loves it."

"I might save her a small bowl."

I chuckle, imagining Blake's reaction to a small bowl of peach cobbler. Neither of us would live through the night.

"We'll be up soon."

Beau salutes and then turns on his heel and walks out. I take a seat on the couch Janie and Mom picked out earlier today and wait for the ladies to finish oohing and ahhing over everything in the building.

I'm about to doze off when Blake sits on my lap, and then

all thoughts of sleep evaporate like the morning dew. She drapes her arms around my neck and leans in close.

"I guess I'll let you slide for carrying me like a sack of potatoes earlier."

"Oh, yeah?"

"Yeah. I mean, you did put in a lot of work here. It's the least I can do."

I stand lightning-quick and sling her back over my shoulder.

"Calvin!" she yells, and I slap her on the ass.

"You were saying?"

"I swear to God, I am going to kick your ass for this." I spin and dump her on the couch and then dart through the front door. "Gotta catch me first."

The sound of her feet slapping the ground behind me pushes me to go faster. I haven't run like this in I don't know how long, and I'm winded before I ever reach the house, but I keep going, knowing she's right on my heels. Just before I reach the safety of the porch, she jumps on my back and propels us both to the ground. I take the brunt of the impact and then roll her off my back and sit across her legs.

"That was a cheap shot, missy." My fingers dig into her sides, tickling up and down her rib cage. She squirms, laughing.

"Stop. Stop. Stop. I take it back."

"What do you say?"

When we were younger, I would hold her down the same way, tickling her until she would scream, "Uncle. Uncle!" Neo makes his way outside to see what all the fuss is about, and when he finds us on the ground, he attacks Blake's face with his tongue.

"Oh, Neo. Gross," Blake says, wiping dog saliva from her

cheek. When I stand, I pull her up with me, and after giving the dog some love, we join the others on the back deck.

"You two done acting like kids? I could use a hand in the kitchen," Mom says, shaking her head at us both, which in turn makes us both laugh.

"I'll help. Just let me wash up first," Blake offers and then follows Mom inside, Neo chasing after her like a lovesick puppy.

"Stay tonight?" I ask as soon as everyone else pulls out of the drive. Spending time with them as a family was nice, but I am beyond ready to have Blake to myself. It's been five days since I've physically touched her, and being around her but not able to show her how much I missed her has been killing me.

"I suppose I could stay . . . if you run me a hot bath and promise to massage my body later. With your mouth."

My cock jumps to attention before she even finishes speaking. I take a step closer to her and grab the hem of her shirt and pull it over her head without taking my eyes off hers. "Would you like that bath before or after?"

"Both?" The simmering fire burning in her gaze is the only invitation I need. My clothes hit the floor the same time hers do, and we meet in a flash of heat. I push against her shoulder, spinning her. Her ass presses against my cock, and I guide it to her slick opening, sliding in with a single stroke.

"Fuck."

She pushes back against me and wiggles her ass. My hands hold tight to her hips, and I slide out slowly, only to slam back into her.

Over and over.

Harder and harder.

Until she shatters around me, screaming out my name in a hoarse, breathless cry of release. The feel of her walls contracting around me pushes me over the final edge, and I fall, my cock twitching and pulsing inside her. I lean over her, my stomach and chest lying across her back, her breasts shoved flat against the kitchen island until my breathing returns to normal and I'm not afraid I'll fall on my ass.

"Fucking hell, Blake." I didn't mean to take her in a fit of passion like a rutting buck. My plan was to make love to her, sweet and slow and filled with all the longing of the last few days. When she stands, she kisses me, her lips pressed to mine, her tongue seeking, searching, and then teasing, until all self-doubt vanishes.

"How about that bath now?"

"I think I can handle that." I take her hand and lead her to the bathroom. After running the hot water a few minutes, I plug the tub and adjust the temperature. "Climb in."

Once she settles in, I sprinkle some scented Epsom salt bath soap into the water since its all I've got, and then I nudge her forward and climb in behind her. The contented sigh that escapes her lips is all the thanks I need. I've spent the last eleven years missing her. I've tried and failed to date other people over the years, always finding something wrong with them, when in reality, there was nothing wrong. They just weren't her. She was it for me. The first, the last, the only.

The ring my mother gave me is stowed away in my sock drawer, but even from that distance, I can hear it calling my name. If it were up to me, I would ask her right here and now to be my wife, but part of loving someone is knowing what is best for them, and I know instinctively that she isn't ready for that. She's on her way, but marriage isn't something you ask of another person until you're both ready. If I asked her now, I would be no different from Brad, trying to tie her down so no one else could have her. And I'd rather be eaten alive by rats than be compared to that slimeball piece of shit.

When the time is right, I'll know. Then, and only then, I will ask her to marry me. And when she says yes, I'll never let her go again.

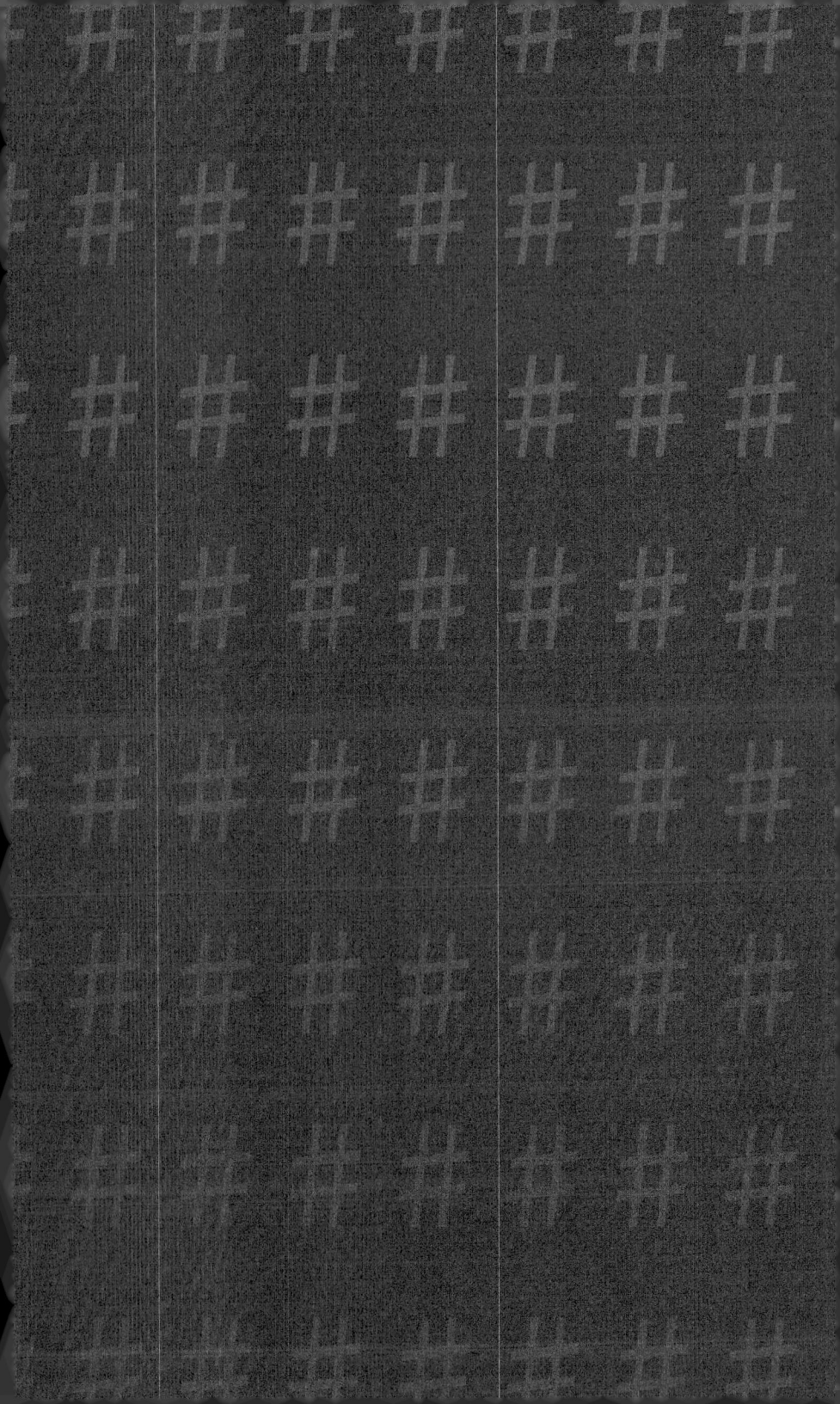

CHAPTER THIRTY FOUR

#morningafter

Blake

MY BODY IS sore in all the right places. When I stretch my arms long, reaching for the ceiling muscle gives way, and the moan that slips from my lips is a testament of the night I had. The space next to me in the bed is empty and cold, but the sweet scent of sausage lets me know that Cal is still in the house. I roll on my side and open my phone, scrolling through notifications, and then I reply to the most important ones.

The house is listed on the market.

Shelly is hiring herself an assistant, and do I know anyone good?

Brad's lawyer has scheduled a conference call for nine AM Central time.

I'm likely to start my period today—that last one came from *Flow*, the app I use to track my cycle.

I click on the link and view my house. The photographer did a great job capturing the space, and then I reply, thanking the agent. My next message is to Shelly. I send her the link and tell her I'll think on the assistant thing for her. She replies with a heart-eyed emoji. I accept the invitation to the conference call and then message Doug and ask him what the plan is. It's fifteen minutes after eight here, which means I have forty-five minutes to prepare.

Breakfast is being plated when I shuffle into the kitchen. My muscles are still warming up. After the aerobic sex last night, it might be a good idea to do some yoga and stretch them out before I try anything more strenuous.

"Morning." I wrap my arms around his torso and lay my head against his naked back. The muscles along his spine bunch when he moves. Neo wakes from his nap on the floor beside his food bowl and begs for attention with a wag of his tail. I leave the warm comfort of Cal and sit on the floor next to him. "Morning to you too, old man."

"He resents that statement. Tell her, Neo. You're not old, are you?"

"The lawyer messaged. I have a conference call this morning."

"About Brad?"

"Yeah. I'm just ready for this to be over. Maybe I should just give him some money and—"

"No. You're not going to be bullied into giving him a damn thing. If you want to out of the goodness of your heart, then fine. I won't tell you what to do or not to do, but I refuse to let him push you to the point of giving up."

"I don't want to. I'm just sick of it all."

"I know, baby, but it will be over soon and you won't ever have to hear his name again." He holds out his hand, and after placing mine in it, pulls me to my feet with a quick kiss on the crown.

"Put some food in your stomach and take a cup of coffee out to the she-shed. You'll have all the privacy you need there."

"The she-shed? Is that what you're calling it?"

"What do you want me to call it? She-shed, Heifer-hut, Bitch-box?"

"How about studio?"

"I guess that works, but Cheryl got a she-shed so I thought you should too."

"Oh, my God. Thanks, Jake from State Farm. Where did you leave your khakis and red button?"

"Get over here and eat, woman." He pulls my arms, dragging me closer.

I shove food into my mouth with the exuberance of a toddler in a highchair with a bowl of spaghetti. Up until then, I hadn't realized how hungry I was. When we finish, I make a cup of coffee and take Cal's advice.

The studio is cool even with the sunlight streaming in. If you walked in, there is no way of knowing this used to be a utility building. They did an amazing job transforming it. Now it resembles a tiny home. After placing my coffee on the table, I light a candle and prepare for the call. Doug messaged me back a list of things we will be discussing and strict instructions on how and when to reply. Basically, if I have a question, I message his cell. When or if an offer is placed on the table, I text him my reply. If I had an extra phone, then I could have muted the conference call on one and kept Doug on the second, but I didn't think about when I was inside and the call is about to start, so I don't have enough time to run back in.

I type in the dial-in number and type in the code to join the chat room. Doug is already in there. The automation asks me my name. That's the first and only thing I will say during this call. Everything else will be communicated by Doug.

I'm in. Going to mute the call so no one hears me cursing, lol
Good idea.

Within five minutes, all parties have joined. Hearing Cindy's voice in the background when Brad states his name takes me off guard. I didn't realize the two were still involved. It reiterates the fact that I was being used and reinforces my desire to make sure Brad doesn't get shit from me.

"My client is willing to settle for three hundred thousand in order to keep the matter from going to court."

No.

"That's a hard no."

"In that case, my client is willing to accept one hundred thousand if he is able to keep the home the couple bought together."

I bought that house.

"I think it's safe to say that we are not willing to accept any settlement. What we are willing to do is discuss the repayment of funds used by your client over the course of four years, including but not limited to the use of my client's credit card accounts and personal checking. If an agreement can be made for the timely repayment, then we are willing to not seek further criminal filings against your client for identity theft as well as theft of property."

"Hold."

What the hell? Can I do that?

We just did.

"My client has advised me that any charges made were during their relationship and not subject to recompensating."

"Your client used federally protected funds via credit cards not in his name. Please advise your client of the law."

"Hold." Brad's lawyer, Mr. Ward, mutes his side of the call so he can discuss how to continue with Brad, who I assume is in the room with him.

"Is your client willing to offer anything for his time and effort put into creating and building the company known as Fresh Start? As a founding member of the company and the person in charge of the daily running, he feels he is owed something." He's reaching for straws now, and everyone on the call knows it, but my heart still skips a beat. My hands shake while I type out the reply.

He didn't.

"We are willing to offer acceptable compensation *if* your client can prove he was a part of the company in any aspect. I have a set of three questions along with the answers I am emailing to you now. If he answers any of them correctly, we can discuss compensation."

Wait, what are you doing? I text Doug frantically.

Don't worry. If he gets any of them right, then I'll personally pay him.

His confidence does little to ease my stress.

"Agreed."

"First question: What date was Fresh Start originally created?"

It takes Brad a few moments to answer. I hear Cindy whisper, and I cringe. "January 2016."

"Second Question: What is Fresh Start?"

"It's a photography company. She takes pictures of people." He's so far off base with this answer. I can't even figure out how he came up with that unless he sees me taking pictures for social media and just assumed I was a photographer. What did he think I went out of town for? Photoshoots?

"Third question: How many employees work for Fresh Start?"

I'm holding my breath now. He's tanked the first two questions, but there is a chance he could know this one. I do most of the company paperwork from my office at home, including the deposit into my Square account for payroll. There are three other ladies who work in the office. One of them handles the timesheets, another weeds through branding consultations, and the last, a young girl we just hired last year, answers all the comments on Instagram and Facebook.

"Three, counting myself."

The pent-up breath I've been holding captive gushes out with the force of a typhoon. He's not getting a dime.

"Mr. Ward, please view the email now, as well as the attachments, and tell me how you would like to proceed."

"Hold."

This time, he is gone longer than any of the others, and I can only imagine the conversation he is having with Brad. When Brad bursts onto the line, I jump and almost pour coffee all over my legs.

"I'll fucking get you for this, Blake. I swear, if it's the last thing I do, you will pay for this shit." A chill snakes down my spine. In four years, I have never heard Brad raise his voice. Not to a stranger, not during rush hour in a fit of road rage, and never to me. Before this moment, I would have been willing to bet an astronomical amount of money on the fact that he wouldn't. I would have lost.

"I have advised my client to drop the case. A formal withdrawal will be filed today. Thank you for your time."

"Thank you."

I disconnect from the conference call and dial Doug's number. He answers on the first ring.

"Hey. Is it over?"

"I'll message you as soon as the withdrawal is filed, but yes, I think it's over."

"How did you know he wouldn't know the answers to those questions?"

"You didn't see the same man we saw every day. He was oblivious to anything except what he absolutely needed to be aware of to keep you. There was never a chance he would get them right."

"Thank you, Doug."

"Anytime, Blake. You take care of yourself."

"You too."

After we disconnect, I take a few minutes to myself, trying to wrap my head around the situation. I don't understand how I could have been so oblivious to the man he was after spending four years with him. Granted, the first year, we weren't living together, but for three of the four years, we were. How did I not realize he cared so little?

Because he said all the right things.

Was I really so easy to fool?

A tap on the door pulls me from my melancholy thoughts. Cal waves through the paned glass and I beckon him inside.

"Are you done?"

"I think so."

"And?"

"He's not getting a penny."

"Then why do you look so glum?"

"I don't know. How did he fool me for so long? Am I self-absorbed? Ignorant?"

"No, you're none of those things. You trusted him, and because you trusted him, you didn't look past what he showed you. You didn't have a reason to."

"I'm usually a much better judge of character. Or at least I thought I was, but I spent four years with a man who was only using me for my money and five years with a best friend who I'm starting to think was in it for the same thing. I heard her in the background on the call, and now I can't help but wonder if it was all a lie."

The thought occurs to me now, and I wonder how I didn't connect it before, but Cindy is the person who introduced me to Brad. She knew what I wanted and needed in a man, and she found me the perfect one. Had they been planning this all along? I think back to the dozens of late-night conversations over ice cream and Moscato. How many times had she asked me why I hadn't married Brad yet? How many times had she pushed the subject?

"I think Cindy may have set me up with Brad so they could both collect. Have they been together this whole time?"

"I don't know, baby, and thinking about it isn't doing you any good. Let it go and be thankful you caught on when you did."

"Yeah." I know he's right, but now that my mind has latched onto the possibility, it won't let go.

"Wait here. I'll be right back."

Distantly, I nod, or at least I think I do. At this point, I don't know who I can trust or what friendships are real. I just handed my company over to Shelly, who I think is a real friend. God knows, she's put in her fair share of work over the years. I want to message her and tell her my suspicions. It's easy to second-guess every decision after this type of betrayal, but in the end, I have to trust in myself.

Do you think Brad and Cindy were a thing before me and him? I'm starting to wonder if this was a scam and they were both in on it.

Oh, snap. Really? I'll do some digging.

Okay. Thanks.

Np. How's everything down there?

It's good. You should come visit when I find a place to live.

Tell me the time and place and I'll be there.

I reply with a wink emoji and then go in search of Calvin.

CHAPTER THIRTY FIVE

#picnic

Calvin

BLAKELYNN'S so distracted she doesn't notice when I leave, but I have the perfect plan to take her mind off everything else for a little while. With the sandwiches made and packed, I head back outside to grab Blake. She's halfway to the house already.

"Come on."

"Where are we going?" she asks.

"A picnic."

"Oh!"

"You can even ride that devil of a stallion if you want."

"I want. I want. I want." She jumps up and down, clapping her hands together.

"Well, get in." Neo races through the yard when I open the

truck's passenger door, leaping into the seat in a single bound. "I guess you can come too, pal."

Blake runs up to her room for a quick change of clothes and to grab her boots. While she's gone, I pull the horses out and start saddling them. It's a miracle, but Samson doesn't pin his ears at me the entire time. When he first arrived, I wasn't sure I'd be able to help him at all. Growing up, I always had an affinity for horses. Even the most aggressive ones tolerated and even liked me, but Samson was an exception. He hated everyone. Then Blake showed up, and since then, he's made a complete one-eighty. She could charm the skin off a snake.

Even on a day like today, when life is beating her down, she still manages to set my soul on fire. "Damn, woman, you are beautiful." Her answering blush sneaks across her high cheekbones. Her lips curve into a sinful smile.

"You're not too bad-looking yourself, cowboy."

"Get your sexy ass on that horse before I decide to take you back inside."

She winks and then double-checks the girth on her saddle. Once she's satisfied with the snug fit, she slips a foot into the stirrup and launches onto Samson's back. *God, her ass in those jeans could kill a man.* "Where to?"

"Do you remember that big oak tree?" The first time we made love was under the canopy of that tree's branches, at dusk, without a care in the world for who saw. Not that anyone was around, but we could have been in a crowded room and not noticed another soul.

Her mouth tilts upward, the ghost of a smile on her lips. "The one by the creek? At the bottom of the hollow?"

"Yeah."

"I remember." And with that, she turns Samson with a tug

of his reins and takes off. Spark and I follow at a distance to begin with, giving Blake space to let Samson work through his excitement. Studs are notorious for having built up stores of energy, and if you're not careful, you'll get a hoof to the shin. He prances to the side and hops, not full-on raring, but lifting his front legs off the ground a little. Blake controls him with little effort, laughing and joking with him the entire time. I take a mental photo of her poised and relaxed smile. Her smiles have been so few since she returned. The stress of the Brad situation has taken more of a toll on her than any of us realized.

"You wanna let him have a little head?" I don't mention that my reason for asking has more to do with the vision of her flying through the air, wind coursing through her hair.

"I think he'd like that."

"Let's go." *Click, click.* Spark stretches out underneath me. His stride elongates, his hoofs beating into the wet grass, *clop, clop, clop.* Once his trot levels out, I tug on the bit and his gait softens into an easy canter.

This right here. This is what I love. It's a part of me, of the essence that makes me who I am. The thought of leaving this behind crushes me, but if the day comes where I have to choose between this and her . . . *I wont lose her again.* This ranch, these horses, the calm serenity of riding across a field at dawn, none of it compares to the way she makes me feel. Half of my life has been without her. Never again.

At the top of the ridge, Blake slows Samson to a gentle walk. Both horses are breathing heavily, a light foam coating their skin. August in Alabama is hotter than the hinges on the gates of hell. Even the trees are looking for shade. Rivulets of sweat pour down my back, soaking my shirt. In the South, the only thing worse than the blazing sun is the skin-melting humidity. You can't walk to the mailbox without needing a shower afterward.

On the other side of the ridge is a hollow, and through it flows chilly creek water. We spent many summers searching for the underground spring that fed this creek, but we never managed to find it. The horses set the pace for descending the rocky hill. I lean back in my saddle and sway left to right with each footfall. When we reach the bottom, I climb off and pull the reins over Spark's head. Neo races toward the creek with a splash. He's never been able to pass up the chance for a swim. I lead Spark to the bank before tying him off under the shade of a giant oak.

"Are you hungry?" The saddle bags are filled with waters and a few cold beers. I hold up one of each, and when she points to the beer, I toss the water back in and grab one for myself.

"I could eat. What did you pack?"

"One ham and one turkey, some cheese, grapes, and a couple of packs of crackers."

"Sounds good."

The small throw blanket I tied to the saddle offers just enough room for us to sit side by side, but at least we're off the grass. I pass her a sandwich, not knowing which one, and then spread out the rest. Neo, on the hunt for a snack, leaves his splashing fun and wanders over to us, stopping every few feet to shake out his fur. Sprinkles of cool water evaporate as soon as they make contact with my skin, but the few seconds are a welcomed refresher.

"I love it here." Blake lies on her back, her hair fanning out around her head. She looks like an angel surrounded by a halo of light. The urge to kiss her consumes me until it's all I can think of, so I lean over and lay my lips against her forehead, her cheek, her lips, her neck, and then repeat. I could die right now a happy man, following the giggle that bursts from her. She reaches for my hand and I give it. I'd give her anything.

Time passes, but neither of us notices. It could have been hours, minutes, days. The sound of thunder rumbling across the cloudless sky brings me back to the present. "Shit." Sitting up, I glance around. Neo is asleep in the grass at the foot of the tree just outside the range of Samson's hooves. Spark is munching on the few leaves he can reach from a low-hanging branch.

"Was that what I thought it was?"

"Yep. We should probably head back." I start to gather up the remnants of our picnic while Blake rolls the blanket back up and attaches it to the saddle. Within minutes, we are loaded up and headed home. I keep an eye on the sky and a tight hand on the reins. Every time a boom shakes the ground, Spark shimmies to the side. He's always been a skittish colt, which is why I try to take him out as often as I can to help him get used to the trail and naturally occurring problems like thunder or a flock of birds taking flight. Samson's doing fine, which surprises me, considering his untrusting nature, but maybe that is only subject to the male species.

We're less than a hundred yards from the barn when the skies part and a flood pours down. Within seconds, I'm soaked through. I tap my heel to Spark's flank and *click-click* him faster. The faster we move, the harder the rain hits. By the time I reach the barn, my flesh feels like I've been shot over and over by a dozen paintball guns.

"Hold on and I'll open the gate." Blake lifts her hand to let me know she heard me rather than trying to yell over the howling wind and rain. Once the gate is opened, we're able to bring the horses inside and get out of the storm. I tie Spark off and then begin unsaddling him. Steam billows from his wet coat. We pushed them hard to make it back here before the storm broke, but even with running full-out, we ended up drenched. The saddle blankets I lay on top of stall doors to dry while Blake pulls the water and feed buckets from two empty stalls so the horses won't eat or drink and get sick before cooling down.

With the horses cared for, we run through the rain to Blake's place in search of dry clothes. The dirt-packed earth is now a mud pit clinging to my boots. Every step is an effort. I make it under the awning before her and spin around, searching through the rain for her. She's laughing and dancing, spinning in circles and leaping through the air like one of the fae folk from the old world. Watching her and hearing her carefree laughter echo over the sound of Mother Nature, I slip, stumble, and fall a little more in love with her.

CHAPTER THIRTY SIX

#youvegotthis

Blake

TODAY, I've decided, is the day I get my shit together, and first on my list of priorities is finding a place to live. The furnishings from my house in Mesa arrived weeks ago and have been gaining dust in a storage unit downtown since. I've licked my wounds enough, and I'm ready.

Sorta.

I don't have the slightest idea where I want to live or how to go about finding something. Should I rent or buy? My mother's house sits empty, a beckoning call in the distant recess of my mind, but the thought of moving in there doesn't sit well with me. I could, at least while I go through everything in the house, but I don't really want to.

Maybe I should start there. I could move priority two into

number one's spot and tackle the job of packing up and cleaning out my mother's belongings. I should have done it ten years ago instead of hightailing it out of town, but after I lost her, I couldn't even walk in her room, much less toss away something. Funny, considering I left it all behind and assumed until a few days ago that it was ruined, trash. I didn't mind it being trashed back then as long as I didn't have to be the one doing the throwing away.

With a clear plan in mind, I call Katherine and ask if she wants to join me. As the closest thing to family we had, a lot of the belongings would mean more to her than Goodwill and I wanted her to have them. She answers on the first ring. If she's surprised by my question, she doesn't show it, and I can't help but wonder if by being unable to deal with this stuff, I have kept her from fully moving on too. Like we're both stuck in the past and desperate to let it go.

Katherine is sitting in a white rocker on the front porch when I pull up. It's the first time I have made the drive down this road on my own since the day I left, and pulling in, seeing her there, I'm overcome with a sense of déjà vu. How many days did I walk down this driveway after school and see this exact scene?

"Hey, I'm glad you could make it."

"Of course I'd be here for this, girl. You shouldn't have to do it alone." Her sun-weathered arms wrap around my neck, pulling me in for a quick hug. "How's that boy of mine treating you?"

"Good. He's always been so good to me."

"He's not too old for me to jerk a knot in his tail if he starts acting up."

Thankfully, Cal leaves the air on in the house even if it's set on eighty. It's a hell of a lot cooler than it is outside. I bump it down a few degrees so we don't sweat to death while we work, and then I lug in a few boxes I picked up at the storage rental place.

"Where should we start?" The house is full, every room bursting with a lifetime's collection of objects.

"That depends on you." I was hoping she had a room in mind and I wouldn't have to make that call, but since she seems content with leaving everything up to me, I head into the living room, dragging boxes along behind me.

"So, what do you think about making four piles? One for you, one for me, one for trash, and the last for donations?"

"Sounds good to me."

After an hour or so of working in silence, I come across Mom's old vinyl player and pop on one of her favorites. Hearing the scratchy tunes of Dolly fill the house again settles my aching spirit. There's not a day that goes by that I won't miss her, but I made us both a promise to never forget her again, and so when Dolly belts out *Jolene*, I stand, and using the small clear vase as a microphone, I sing the lyrics at the top of my lungs. Halfway through, Katherine joins me, and by the time the song finishes, neither of us has dry eyes. For the first time since losing her, I can feel my mother by my side, laughing and singing along. My soul is at peace, and another of the cracks in my heart fills in, covered by the glue of new memories and old uniting.

It's after dark by the time we finish for the day. After finishing the living room, we moved on to the kitchen and then the guest room. The number of boxes for Goodwill outnumbers the boxes we want to keep three to one, but I'm still surprised by the boxes full of items I couldn't part with.

"'Tomorrow? Same time?" Katherine asks before climbing into her S10.

"I'm meeting with the new team members tomorrow and need to get them started on the trails, but I should be here by noon. The key is under the pot if you decide to come earlier."

"Sounds good. You be safe headed home."

"You too."

On the way home, I stop and pick up a pizza then text Cal to see if he wants to join me for dinner.

I already ate, but I'm down for dessert. He replies, followed by a winky face. Incorrigible.

See you in five.

What can I say? I'm a simple girl with simple girl needs.

Feed me.

Love me.

I don't require much else, but if he's offering, you can bet your buttered biscuit I'm gonna show up.

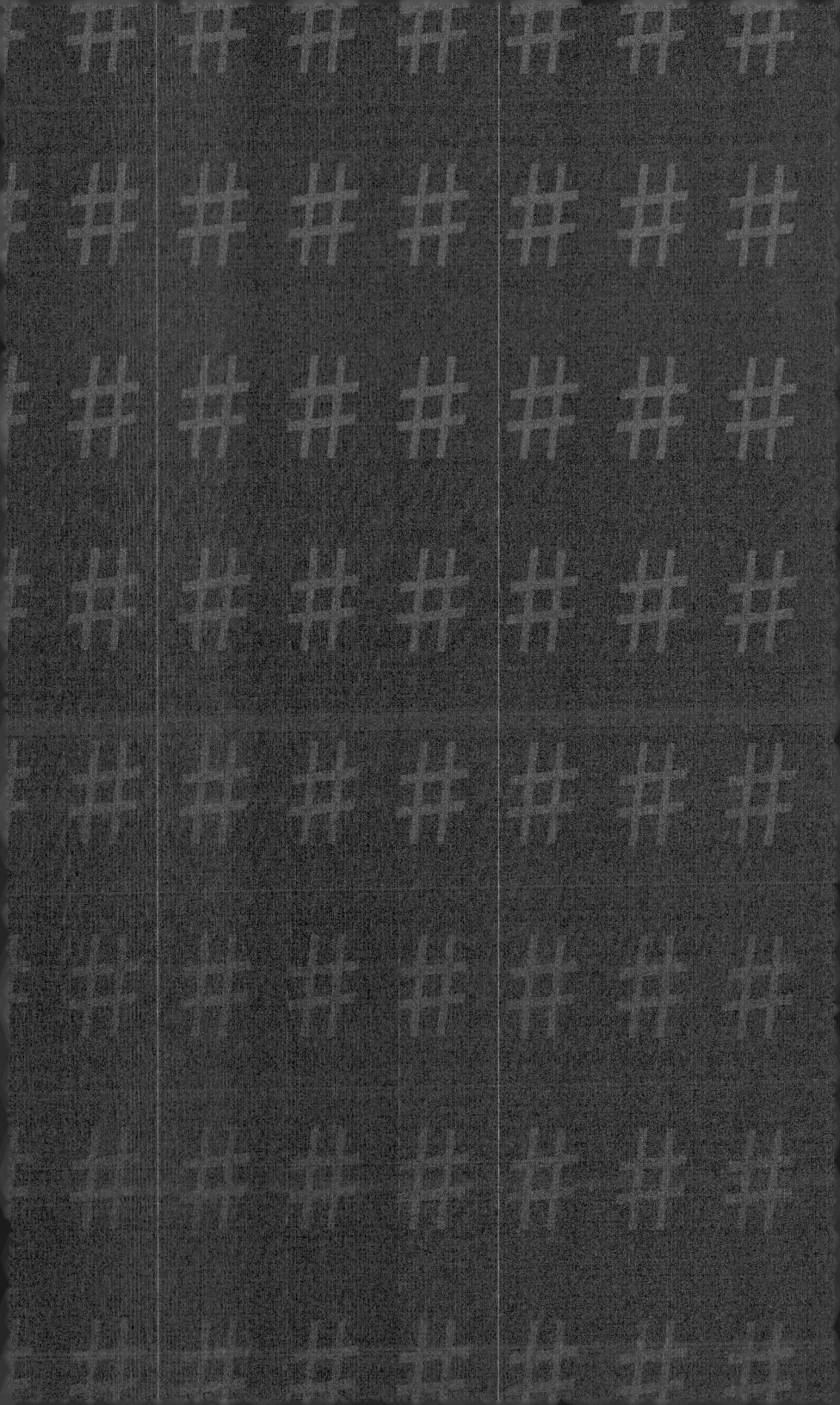

CHAPTER THIRTY SEVEN

#whatthehell

Calvin

THE NEXT MORNING, Blake is sleeping so hard I don't bother waking her. We were up half the night eating pizza and watching reruns of some chick flick show about doctors. I couldn't get into it but I liked being there when Blake started crying over something happening.

I wouldn't have left her at all this morning, but I'd put in an order for feed a few days ago and got a call yesterday that it would be ready at seven, so I slipped from bed, fed the horses, and hopped in my beat up pickup. If I were lucky, I could pick up the feed and make it back before Blake woke up.

When I pull into J&J's Feed, the yard is full of trucks backed to the door. I step out of the cab and make my way inside.

"Hey, Cal. I've got your order ready. Just pull on a door as soon as one clears."

"No problem, Jay. Take your time." Three hours and twenty-seven minutes later, I'm loaded down and on my way.

I smell the sweet tang of smoke before I see it. When I finally find the source, my heart stops beating. I hit the gas. The truck bounces across a pothole and slides to a stop in the gravel outside the barn.

"Blake!" I yell, racing to the front. I can't see past the flame and smoke. Samson kicks the walls of his stall, and I know, the way I know this fire isn't natural, that Blake is inside. She wouldn't have left Samson in there. She would risk her own life to save the smallest animal. There's no way she'd leave him.

I know I'm right when I see the rest of the stall doors open, including Samson's. But the damn devil of a horse won't leave Blake. The smoke is thicker inside. I pull off my shirt and cover my face while pulling on Samson's halter. When I get him out of the stall, I smack him hard on the ass. He shoots past the smoke and flames into the fresh, clear air.

My eyes are burning, but I don't stop searching.

"Blake! Blake! Can you hear me?"

"Calvin? Blake?" I hear Beau outside now, and in the distance, the sound of sirens.

"I'm here. I can't find Blake," I yell back at him, and then I hear a whimper from the corner. I wave my hands through the air and crouch down, searching with my arms stretched in front of me.

I could pass out in relief when I feel her, but she isn't moving and the relief I feel vanishes. I pull my shirt from my face and wrap it around hers before picking her up and trying to find my way out. If I hadn't spent every day for the last few years here, I might not be able to find the door, but I know this barn inside out. I could navigate it in the dark, so I shut my eyes and put one foot in front of the other, following the sound of Beau's voice.

When I clear the door, he takes Blake from me and I fall to the ground in a fit of coughing. I try to track them but my eyes burn so badly I can barely see three feet in front of me. I hear them, though. The volunteer fire department made it before the city. Mark, the chief, is shouting for oxygen and radioing in for an ambulance.

I pull myself to my knees and then my feet. I need to get to her. She'll be scared and alone, and she needs me. I take a step and stumble.

"Hey, I got ya."

"I need her."

"She's gonna be okay, man. You saved her. Now let's get you looked at."

"I need her," I say, trying to pull away, but my legs won't carry me on my own.

"All right, all right, I'll take you over, but we have to get you checked out. You're losing a lot of blood."

I don't feel the pain until he says that, and then that's all I feel.

"My back."

"Yeah, you got a pretty bad cut there. Don't worry, the ambulance is on the way. We'll get you taken care of."

When we reach the rig, Blake is sitting up, fighting against Beau, who's trying to hold her in place and force her to take oxygen. "I need to see Calvin. Let me go, Beau, or I swear to God, I will murder you in your sleep."

"Fucking hell, Blake. What do you think he will do to me if

I let you go? Either way, I'm fucking dead. Now sit down and let me help you."

I would laugh if I thought I wouldn't die. As it is, I stumble across the yard and barely make it her side. "Calvin. Are you okay? God, I thought I lost you. I can't lose you, Calvin. Not now. Not ever again."

"I'm fine. I'm okay," I tell her, and then, unable to stand for a second longer, I fall to the ground. Everything after is a blur as I float in and out of consciousness, but I hear Blake threatening the lives of several other people. I could be hallucinating, but I think I hear her tell me she loves me.

CHAPTER THIRTY EIGHT

#youcanttakehim

Blake

I CAN'T LOSE HIM. I just got him back. I don't know how to even process the thought of losing him. I can't see a future without Calvin. I don't care how cheesy it sounds or what anyone in this whole damn world thinks about it. I need him the way a drowning man needs air.

I tried to live without him before. I had myself convinced I was happy and that life was good. In a lot of ways, it was, but I wasn't happy. I didn't even know what happy was. He made me want to kill him almost daily. He was arrogant and cocky. He thought he knew everything and treated me like someone who needed to be protected and worshiped when I wanted to be treated like an equal, but he's my best friend.

My soulmate.

"I can't lose him," I say again and again, rocking back and forth in the hard plastic hospital chair. They rushed Calvin back to surgery to stop the bleeding over an hour ago, and so far, no one has come out to update us. My mind is running amuck, playing out ten thousand different possible reasons. Logically, I know it means they're working. I mean, I've seen enough *Grey's Anatomy* to know as long as the doctor doesn't come out, everything is fine. Right?

But knowing something and telling my heart to believe something are two totally different things. Every time the doors open, I flinch.

"He's not going anywhere. Cal's too damn hard-headed to let a little cut keep him from you."

I try to smile my thanks, but I'm afraid it comes out more of a grimace. News of the fire spread like . . . well, like wildfire. The local station reported on the incident, and since I had been promoting Point of Retreat on my personal account, someone from Arizona had grabbed the story. My phone hadn't quit going off with notifications, so I finally muted them all and laid it facedown. I wanted to pick it up now and waste time on social media scrolling, but I didn't want to see all that again.

We weren't sure what caused the fire. The police had been here to interview me twice in the last hour. I don't think I was very helpful during the first interview, so they came back for another. I didn't have much to tell them. No, I hadn't noticed anything strange. No weird smells or noises, except for Samson going a little crazy, stomping and kicking his stall. He hadn't acted like that since I first rescued him back in Arizona, and usually, only when a man was around.

But I had been alone, working on cleaning out the stalls and putting down fresh shavings after I got the boys started marking off and cleaning up the trails this morning. Until I smelled the smoke. I had let all the other horses out earlier, except for Sammy, so I could come and go in their stalls without fear of them getting out, but since he was a stud, it was hard to let him out with the others.

I didn't want him fighting or getting hurt trying to befriend a mare.

I stepped out of the stall to try and find the smoke when I saw the fire. My first instinct was to get Samson out.

Everything after that was a blur. The next thing I fully remember was fighting Beau and trying to get to Calvin.

Now he was in surgery, and I was waiting, slowly losing my mind.

"How much longer can it take" I ask no one in particular. The waiting room had slowly filled over the last thirty minutes. Half of them were people I didn't recognize and the other half, I had seen around town. A few of the students who were recruited for the new 4H program stopped by but left again while I wasn't paying attention.

"Beau? Blake?" I hear my name and lift my head. Katherine, Cal's mom, is standing at the entryway, searching the room. I untangle my arms from my legs and stand.

"Over here."

She hurries to the corner we've cleared out and claimed as our own. "Any word yet?"

"No. and every time we try to ask for an update, they say they can only release that information to family."

"Well, if you two aren't family, who is?" I shrug my shoulders and pull my legs back into the seat with me.

"Let me see what I can find out." I nod my head and resume rocking. Katherine eyes me for a second before pulling

Beau to the side. I can't hear what she says to him, but he shakes his head back and forth and then sits back down next to me.

"He's going to be fine."

I hope he's right. I need him to be right.

An hour, a second, a week. I don't know how much time has passed before Katherine returns. I've been lost in the violent circle of my own thoughts. It's not until I register the smile on her face that my mind stops screaming at me.

"What?" I ask.

"He's out. Everything went great. He's in recovery now and will be moved to a room in the next hour."

I let out a shaky breath and then choke on it as tears clog my throat. I don't want to cry. I never cry. It's one thing I'm most proud of.

"They said only one person can visit in recovery. I think you should go."

"Me?" Surely, I heard her wrong. She should go. He's her son, after all.

"Yes, go and see him for yourself. He's okay, Blake."

"But..."

"Blakelynn Smith, get your ass out of that chair and go check on my son."

I stand. "Yes, ma'am." As I make my way toward the hall leading out of the waiting room, I hear her call out.

"Room 6410."

Calvin is still hooked to oxygen when I enter. There are several other lines coming and going from his body, IVs and whatnot, but he is awake.

I take a step into the room and stand next to the bed. I don't want to touch him and hurt him, but I need to know he's okay.

His eyes search my face, my body, checking me over. I try to smile and reassure him.

"Hey." My whisper sounds like a trumpet blaring. It's so quiet in here, the only sounds the beeping of the monitor and the oxygen blowing. It hurts to see him like this. Almost as much as it hurt to see my mother in the same position.

Broken.

And knowing there was nothing I could do to help.

"Hey." His voice is muffled through the mask. His hand lifts to pull it down, and I reach for it to help him. He coughs a little, and I try to shove it back on his face, but he pushes my hands away. "Are you all right? I was so worried."

I laugh at that. "I'm fine. Thanks to you."

"What happened?" he asks, and I shake my head. I wish I knew.

"I don't know. It started out of nowhere. One minute, I was shoveling manure and the next, the barn was up in flames."

"The horses?" he asks.

"All fine. Samson too. Thank you for getting him out."

"Stubborn ass animal. He didn't want to leave you."

"How do you feel?" I ask.

"Good now that you're here."

"That's not what I meant."

"Blake. I can't lose you again."

"Cal..."

"You're so bright and shiny."

"Cal, I think you're still high from pain meds." He reaches, trying to pick something from the air around me, but grabs my shirt sleeve instead. When he pulls, I fall forward across him. I try to catch myself and save him from the weight of my body crushing his injuries.

"I wish you knew how much I love you."

I push up on my hands and then my elbows. I fight the desire to meet his gaze. Fight and lose. But when I lift my eyes, his are closed. A soft snore escapes, and I lift the oxygen mask back to his face while trying to process his words.

I wish you knew how much I love you.

I can't. It's too much, too soon.

CHAPTER THIRTY NINE

#whathappened

Calvin

WHEN I WAKE, the room is full. Blake is in the corner of the window seat, curled into herself. My mother sits in the only chair, watching my bed for any sign of life. She jumps to her feet when she notices my eyes opening.

"Well, about time." I grimace. "Are you in pain?" She asks and presses the button to call for the nurse.

"No. I'm fine."

"Nonsense. You just had surgery. Don't try to ignore it. Take the meds they offer."

"Okay, Mother."

"I'm going to grab a bite from the cafeteria. Does anyone want anything?" she asks. Blake shakes her head no.

"I'll walk down with you. I could use some coffee," Beau

says, standing and opening the door to the room. Mom follows him out after one more glance in my direction, and then it's only me and Blake left. She climbs down from the window seat when the room clears and sits on the edge of my bed.

"How are you feeling, really?" she asks.

"My side hurts like a bitch, and my stomach keeps growling, but other than that, I'm okay."

"I can grab you something to eat. They brought in a tray of food earlier, but you were knocked out. I had the nurse take it away after an hour or so. Figured you didn't need salmonella on top of major surgery."

"Right now, all I want is you. Crawl in here with me." I pull back the blanket and scoot over as much as I can without falling off the bed.

"Okay, but if it hurts, you let me know and I'll get up." I nod my head in agreement, but the truth is I would endure any amount of pain to feel her body next to mine. For a moment, when I found her laying lifelessly on the ground, I thought she was dead. I didn't know how I would continue living without her.

I never planned on Blake coming back home. As far as I knew, she was happy in Arizona and planned to stay there for the rest of her life. But she did come back, and now I don't think I can live my life without her in it. While I'm busy trying to find the words to say, Blake has fallen asleep.

It had to be a hard night for her. We lived in the hospital for years when her mom was sick, worrying every day that it would be the last, afraid to run home and grab more clothes. In the end, no amount of hoping, praying, or wishing could keep her here. I couldn't imagine the loss or pain she felt. Even though I was close to Tricia, I wasn't her child.

I'm surprised Blake even stepped foot in here, much less stayed all night. When Mom and Beau walk back in the room, another woman follows them. I hold up my finger to my lips and point down at Blake sleeping. Mom smiles, brushing Blake's hair from her face.

"She hasn't slept."

"I figured," I reply and glance at the other woman raising my eyes in a silent question.

"Oh, yeah, this is Shelly. We found her wandering around, looking for Blake."

Shelly steps closer, holding out her hand. I take it without a thought and shake. "Hi, nice to meet you. I've heard lots of great things about you all."

I still don't follow completely, a fact Beau seems to take notice of.

"Shelly was Blake's assistant back in Arizona."

"Oh, yeah." I remember where I'd heard the name now. Blake was just telling me about making Shelly her CEO of the marketing company. She had been worried how to settle things there in order to move back here permanently, and the last month of having Shelly handle business had given her the answer she needed.

"Is everything okay?" I ask, concerned and wondering whether I should wake Blake.

"Oh, yeah, everything is fine with the company. I'm here for her. I . . . well, I guess at this point, the whole country has heard about the fire. I wanted to come and make sure she was all right."

"Oh. That's good." I don't know what to make of her comment about the whole country hearing about the fire. I don't even understand how that is possible, but I'm too tired to ask. The nurse walks in with my dinner tray and a cup of pills. I'm not sure which one I'm more excited for. My stomach rumbles, answering the question for me. I reach for the tray and open it, filling the room with scents of baked chicken and steamed cabbage. The nurse passes me the cup of pills, explaining each one to me. I barely hear her. Tilting back a pink cup of water, I toss the pills in my mouth and swallow then grab my fork and take a bite.

 Nothing has ever tasted so good.

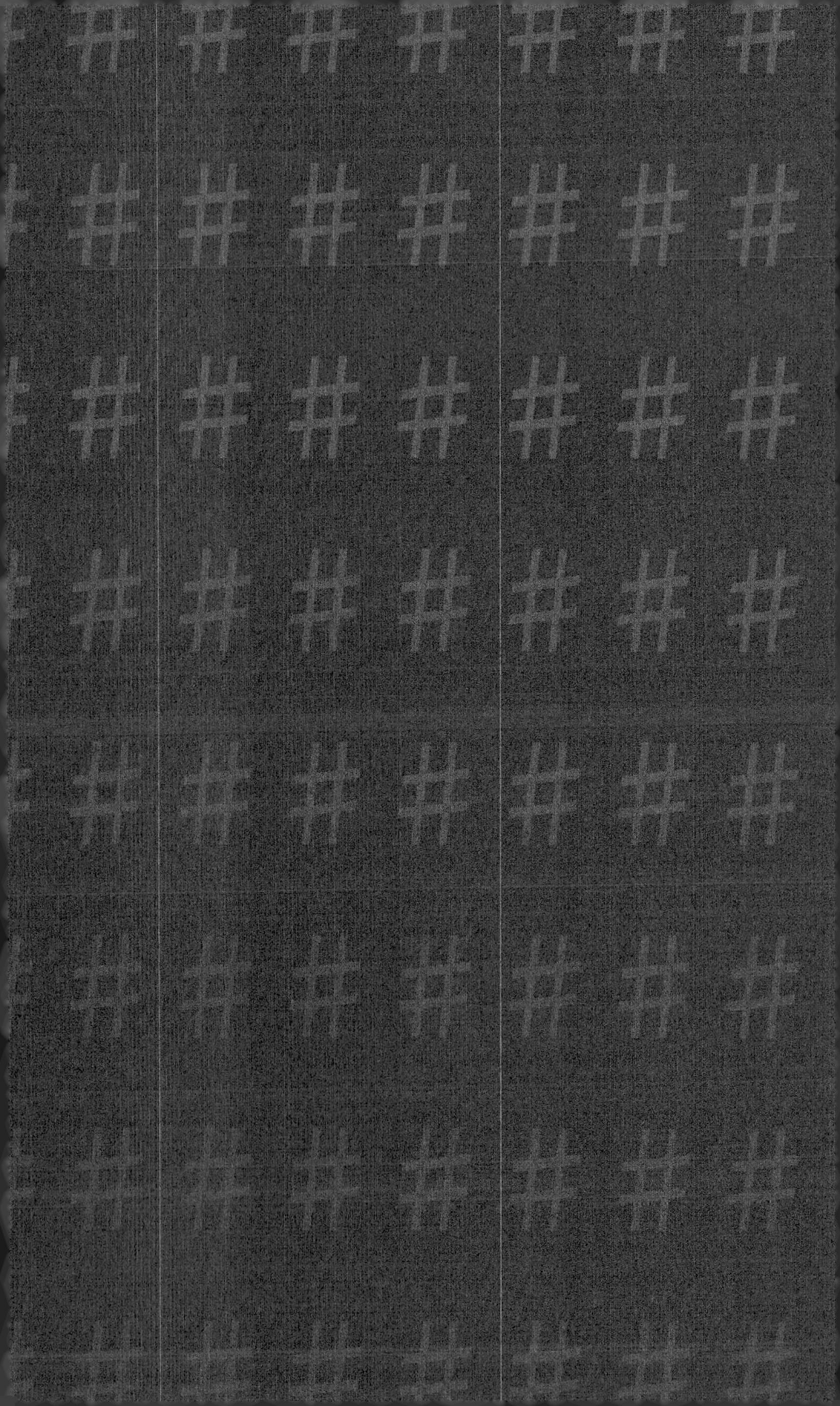

CHAPTER FORTY

#greatnews

Blake

"I STILL CAN'T BELIEVE IT." I hear Calvin before opening my eyes. I can't believe I fell asleep curled next to him on this tiny hospital bed, but my body and mind were exhausted and apparently needed the reboot.

"I think it's amazing." I recognize that voice. Sitting up, I glance around the room. Shelly is sitting on the couch with Beau, her computer open, pointing out something. I pat my head, trying to tame the mess of hair I'm sure is sticking out everywhere.

"Morning, sleepyhead. Look who we found."

"Shelly?" Obviously, it's her, but I'm still trying to process seeing her here.

"Hey, you."

"What are you doing here?"

"I came to check on you. And then these two wouldn't let me leave."

"What are y'all looking at?"

"Oh. So, word of the fire got out, and you know how people can take something and run with it. Well, someone, I'm not sure who yet, decided to start a volunteer page to help rebuild the barn. But that's not even the best part. Not only have hundreds of people volunteered, but companies across America have donated to the cause. Everything is completely financed."

"Really?" I ask, reaching for the laptop and scanning the page. "Wow."

"And the best part—remember that idea you had a few weeks ago?" Beau asks, and I search my mind, going over every idea I've gone to him and Cal with over the last month until I snag on one in particular.

"The rehab?" I ask.

He nods his head. "Fully funded."

My hand covers my mouth, tears filling my eyes. "No way."

"Yep, now all we need is your okay to move forward."

"My okay?" I ask.

"It was your idea. Your baby. It's yours if you want it."

"I want. Hell, yes, I want!"

I turn to Calvin, who's just been watching the play by play, and wrap my arms around him, careful not to hurt him. A month ago, I thought I knew the path I wanted my life to take. I had everything mapped out, a detailed plan. I was going to change the world. And then Brad and Cindy happened. I wasn't sure how to move past that. It shook me to my core and not because he cheated. Men can be pigs. I knew that.

I was shaken because everything I believed, everything I

preached to others, came crashing down around me. I struggled with the decision to leave Arizona and then struggled some more when I decided to come back home to Alabama. It felt like I was running away, and I wanted the world to know I'm not a quitter. I don't run. Not anymore.

Then I got here, and for the first time in years, the constant need to succeed, to push on, to fight and conquer vanished. I took my first real breath in a lifetime and just lived in the moment. One moment, followed by another and another. There have been tons of ups and downs, but at the end of the day, I know this is where I'm supposed to be.

And now, new dreams are growing, and from them, wonderful things are sprouting and blossoming into a life full of wonder and possibilities. A life full of happiness.

CHAPTER FORTY ONE

#hearttoheart

Calvin

I GET to go home today. Fucking finally. I was starting to worry they weren't ever going to release me. Who the hell decided you had to piss and crap before being discharged? I cut my side open and punctured my spleen, not my ass. As far as I'm concerned, everything is still working fine. It doesn't have any reason not to.

Beau's giving me a ride back to the ranch. He seems to find it funny that I'm being wheeled downstairs in a wheelchair, but I tried to fight them on it and walk out on my own, only for them to tell me I can't leave. Rules, rules, and more rules. None of which make a bit of sense.

"Can you climb in on your own, or do you need a boost?"

"Fuck you."

"What squirrel crawled up your ass?" he asks

"Shut the hell up." Thankfully, he does just that.

"Where's Blake?"

Beau swipes his fingers across his lips, miming his vow of silence.

"What are you, twelve?" I ask, trying not to laugh.

"I don't know where she is. She's been tied up for a few days with Shelly, coordinating the rebuild activities."

"Hmmph."

"Trouble in paradise?" he asks, and I side-eye him, wondering how much I should say.

Screw it.

"Has she been acting weird? I mean, when she comes around, she seems distant or something."

"Nah. She seems fine to me."

"So, it's just me she's weird with. Great."

"Maybe she just freaked after the hospital thing. You know she hates that place."

"Maybe," I say slowly. That's a good point, but I don't think so. "I think it's got more to do with the fact that I told her I loved her."

"You what?"

I let out a deep breath and hunch my shoulders. "Yeah," I say sheepishly.

"Shit."

"Now I just need to figure out how to fix it."

It's like one minute, she is fine. She's wrapping her arms around me and falling asleep in my bed, and the next, she remembers my drug-induced confession and starts pulling away. She gets twitchy and her mind short-circuits. I make a plan to corner her and get to the bottom of this.

When we round the drive, I'm surprised by the number of cars. I didn't realize they were starting rebuilding efforts this soon. After closer examination, I see they are cleaning the site up. Just thinking about the years of collecting equipment that was lost in the blaze makes my stomach twist and roll.

I'll never be able to rebuild it all.

I climb from the truck and sidestep people, making my way to Beau's porch. I wanted to walk through the barn and survey the damage for myself, but I don't want to do it with an audience.

Blake is sitting at the kitchen table when I step in. I startle her when I slam the door. "Hiding from the crowd?" I ask, pulling out a chair.

"Yes. No. I don't know anymore."

"What's wrong?"

"The sheriff just left. They know how the fire started."

"Oh, good. Right?" I ask and then take the time to really look at her. "Or not?"

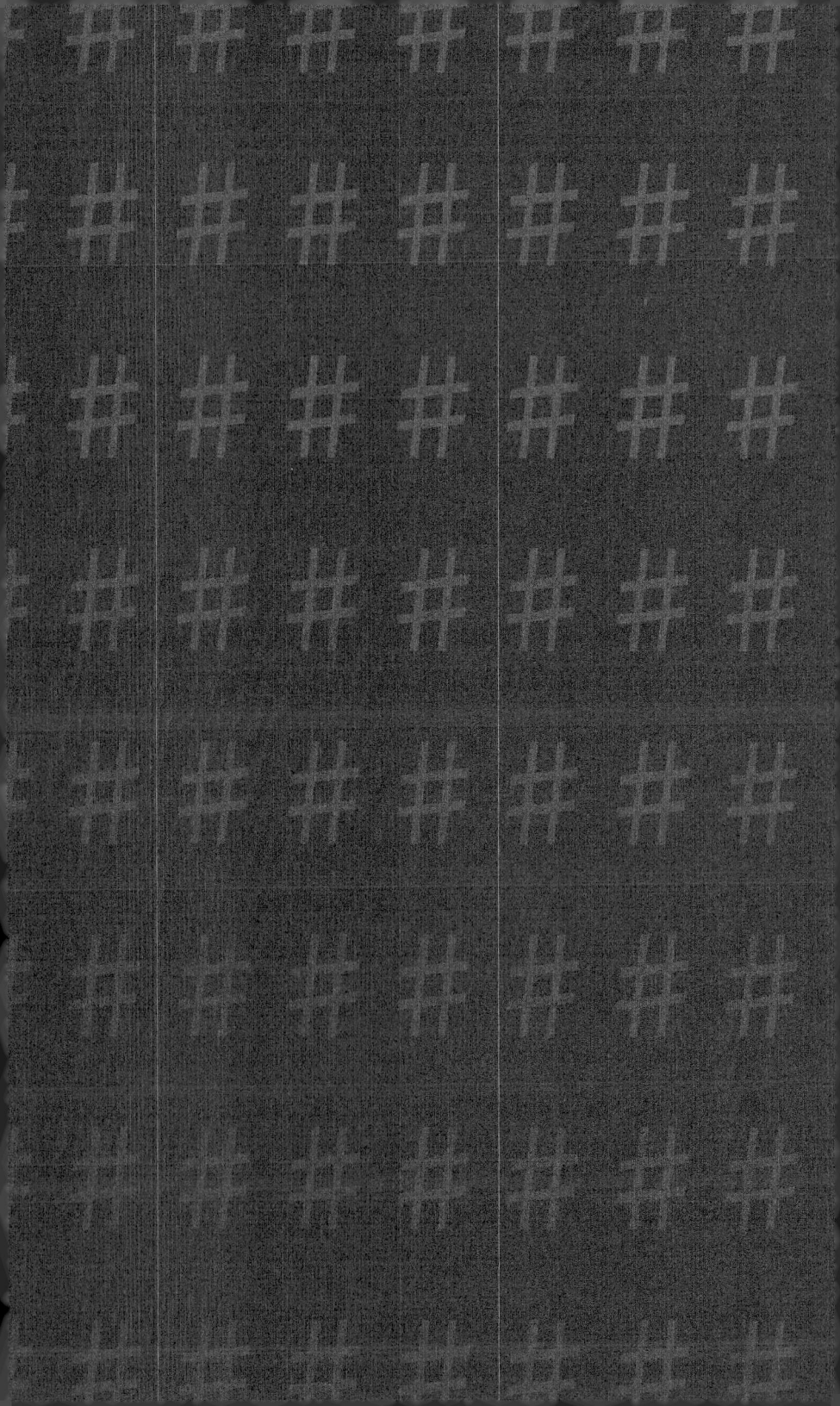

CHAPTER FORTY TWO

#jailtime

Blake

"BRAD WAS ARRESTED THIS MORNING." My hands are still shaking, and it's been hours since the call. My mind, still dazed, is having the hardest time understanding how the person I spent four years with could do this to me. *And Cindy . . .* I couldn't even think about her.

"Brad? The douche canoe ex?" Calvin says, and I can see the gears turning, his mind trying to catch up.

"One and the same."

"Okay, I'm going to need you to back up and explain."

"Apparently, he took out a life insurance policy on me when I accepted his proposal. I didn't even know you could do that—take out a policy on someone who isn't related to you."

I still can't fully wrap my head around it all.

"Anyway, he took out a policy in the event of my death, and yesterday morning, he contacted the company to file a claim. I'm not sure how it all got pieced together, but from what I can gather, he was pissed he didn't win anything in the lawsuit, and he went with the next option, which was to kill me off and collect.

"Except I didn't die. Because you pulled me from the fire. So, when he tried to file a claim, they investigated and found me alive and well. After verifying that I didn't die, they contacted the authorities. He's being held on attempted murder, arson, and fraud."

And now we know the truth. Calvin almost died because of me. If I hadn't come back here, hadn't brought my drama here, then he would never have been hurt trying to save my life. Everything he had worked his life away for wouldn't be destroyed—gone in the flames lit by my money-hungry ex.

How could I have spent four years with someone and not realized he was capable of murder? Or better yet, that he only wanted me for the money I brought to the table? Am I so flawed that I can't recognize that level of darkness in someone? Cindy is being investigated too. I'd forgotten about her, but Shelly reminded me of a conversation we had a few weeks ago, and I relayed the information to the Sherriff. Two people I trusted, that I cared for. I thought cheating was bad, but this . . . this is the ultimate betrayal. A part of me wishes I had just given him the money he asked for. Then maybe . . .

"This isn't your flaw. You don't get to take the blame for this. This is all Brad." I don't realize I spoke the last sentence aloud until Calvin responds. I wish I could believe his words. I wish I could trust my own instincts, but after all this, I think it's fair to say my instincts suck ass.

How the hell am I supposed to trust that the love I feel for Calvin is true, that it is good? That it is what I need? How can I move forward knowing that my presence in his life almost caused him to lose his life? I am the toxic person in this relationship. Everything I touch is ruined.

"Blake." Calvin's voice is calm. It quiets the anxiety building in my mind.

"Yeah?" I answer remorsefully and ready to flee.

"I can see your thoughts written across your face like a book."

"Then you know it's true." I should go. It doesn't matter that I love Calvin or that I have found my place here. My presence endangers the people I care about, and that isn't something I'm okay with.

"Bullshit. Brad is a lemon. He sucks major ass, but he's just a lemon. If you buy a car and it turns out to be a lemon, do you hate all cars after that? No, because not all cars are bad. Do you quit driving altogether because you chose a car that was a lemon? No. Of course not. How were you supposed to know? Right?"

"Okay. I think I'm following you."

"Brad is a lemon. You didn't know it when you chose him. He didn't come with a sticker, and you chose to take him home anyway. He was packaged perfectly. Nice, shiny, and new, and then one day, he turned to shit. You don't give up because you got a lemon, baby. You trade that fucker in."

"And I trade Brad in on . . ."

"On me, obviously. I'm more of blackberry. I can grow and adapt in any condition and I never give up. I can be thorny, but if you take the time to try to see past all that, I'm a really juicy mouth of yum."

I toss back my head and laugh. I can't help it. And then I stand and take the two steps that separate us and sit in his lap, wrapping my arms around him and inhaling his scent. This man could charm a rattlesnake if he wanted to. And I love him. I let that sink in for a second. I love Calvin Hunt, and I don't want to run from him again. I don't want to run ever.

"You don't smell like a blackberry," I say, sniffing along his collar bone. My lips press to the soft spot under his ear.

"No? what do I smell like?" he asks.

"Mine," I reply.

EPILOGUE
#gotthegirl

Calvin

THINGS WITH BLAKE and me have sorted out and I couldn't be happier. I think she took to heart my comments when I was being ridiculous and calling myself a blackberry. But it's the truth. Every single word.

The injuries I sustained in the fire are healing nicely, as is the rebuild to the ranch. I still can't believe that all the people who came and donated their time and money were mostly due to the work Blake was doing. It never seemed like she was doing a lot, always talking to the faceless people through her computer or taking and posting photos. But the impact of this social media and her followers has been significant. She says that coming home for her was like taking her first breath of fresh air in eleven years. Her coming back breathed life back into us and the ranch.

Beau's taken to all the changes like a duck to water. It's helped, having Shelly around for those few weeks, taking the time to explain things to him and show him in more detail the impact we're having. I'm grateful for that. I'm also grateful for having Blake around, helping me during my convalescence. Once she got over the bullshit that was going through her head that she was the harbinger of doom, she admitted that I, Neo, and Samson were family and that she'd stick around.

And so she should. I'm not planning on going anywhere, but had she up and left as she was known to do, I would have upped my sorry ass to follow her. No way in hell am I going to let her get away this time.

I look around the ranch at all the preparation that's gone into tonight. The setting sun, with streaks of burnt orange and red in the sky, provides the most perfect backdrop for what I have planned tonight. My hand subconsciously pats my front pocket. I feel the hard square bulge and smile. Tonight is the night, and finally, I know she's ready, just as I know I am. I've been ready for half my life. Sometimes, things don't work out the way we plan them because it's not the right time or person or place.

I've always known Blake was it for me, but I had to wait for her. I would do it all again, if need be. She's meant to be my forever. My always.

She is my home.

With an apple in hand, I walk up and coax Samson into coming to me. I must be doing okay since he seems to have mellowed when I'm around. I think on some level, he knows what I did to save Blake. He lets me place the bridle and harness around his neck. I murmur encouragingly to him. He'd better not screw up my plans tonight. I think he'll be fine, and the risk of harnessing him to the small wagon will be worth it to see Blake's face when he trots up to her.

After all, this evening's outing is sort of her idea, anyway. She's the one who wanted to offer up experiences at the ranch for things like engagements and weddings. This will be the first sunset tour in the fields, and I hope that by the end of the evening, I can officially call her mine.

"Are you ready?" Beau asks, stepping around the corner.

"Yeah. Does Mom have Blake distracted?"

"Yeah, they're going through photo albums."

"Okay." I duck under Samson's thick neck and pass the reins to Beau. "I'm going to text Mom and tell her to make an excuse to come out here. Y'all head over to the spot we picked out, and then I'll grab Blake. Remember to stay hidden. But don't spook this beast."

"Gotcha." He claps me on the shoulder. "Good luck."

"Thanks, man."

After double-checking the wagon for supplies, I text my mother, and then when she and Beau disappear across the field, I text Blake.

I've got a surprise for you. Walk outside.

I wait a minute after the message shows as read and then I click my tongue and steer Samson toward the house.

Her eyes widen when she steps out the door, and then a smile as bright as the sun lights her face.

"Come on, lets go for a ride."

"How did you do this?"

"Well, first, you hook the leads to the wagon and then—" Her fist hits me in the shoulder and I lean to the right in exaggerated pain. "Is that how to treat a man who surprises you with gifts? Damn, woman."

"You know what I meant."

"Yeah, but I can't give away all of my secrets, now can I?"

This time when she raises her arms, instead of hitting me, she wraps them around my neck and pulls me in for a kiss. "Ready for a ride?" I ask.

"Hell, yeah."

I send up a silent prayer that Samson cooperates and then together, we make our way across the fields.

"This would be so perfect for a wedding," Blake comments, glancing around. The sun is on its final descent across the mountains in the distance.

"I know. Believe it or not, I was paying attention to you when you droned on and on."

"I'm starting to think you like me hitting you."

My stomach is rolling the closer we get to the meeting spot. No words form, and even if they did, I don't think I could push them out right now. When the wagon rolls to a stop, I step down and then offer my hand to Blake. As soon as her feet touch the ground, I reach into my pocket and pull out the ring box. Dropping to one knee, I open the box and ask the most important question of my life.

"Blakelynn Smith, from the time I could walk, I've loved you. For me, there will never be another. I want all of my arguments and all of my achievements to be shared with you. I want you for the rest of my life. Will you marry me?"

Her eyes, which until now were dry and clear, are now filled with the glistening of tears. One hand is pressed to her mouth, the other wrapped around her stomach. I hold my breath, waiting. When she nods her head, I almost fall to the ground, the relief is so great. "Yes. Yes, I will marry you."

Pulling her mother's ring from the box, I take her hand in mine and slide it over her ring finger. I stand and pull her into my arms. In the distance, I can hear my mother crying and the click of the camera, but I can't take my eyes off Blake. She holds her hand up, checking out the ring. I see the flash of awareness when she realizes what ring it is.

"Calvin? Is this . . . ?" Her voice trails off as tears stream down her cheeks.

"Yes. It's your mother's. She left it to my mom for you."

Her arms wrap around my neck again, and this time, her body shakes with joyous sobs. "Thank you."

I don't know why she's thanking me. It should be the other way around. I plan to spend the rest of my life showing her how grateful I am to spend my forever with her.

Beau and Mom join us, popping the bottle of champagne and pouring each of us a glass. We stand under the setting sun, arms locked with our family, and toast to the future. I pull my mom in for a hug and thank her once again for everything. I wouldn't be the man I am today without her love, and I damn sure wouldn't have been able to make this day nearly as special without her support. I don't know what the future holds for any of us. The ranch is headed in a whole new direction with the new barn and stables. Life is speeding toward us. But I know that no matter what, everything will be fine.

"Last one back to the barn is a roasted duck," Blake says, jumping into the wagon's seat.

"Oh, no, you don't. I took amazing pictures of your engagement. The least you can do is give an old man a ride back to the house," Beau says, climbing onto one of the two benches lining the wagon.

"Same. Although I didn't take pictures, but I created that," Mom says, pointing at me.

"Fine, everyone in. But I'm driving," Blake says, taking the reins in her hand. I hop up next to her before I get left behind. The ride back is jarring but filled with the laughter of friends and family. It's a memory I will treasure for the rest of my life.

"Who is that?" Blake asks when the barn comes into view. A woman stands on Beau's front porch, her hands on her hips and a scowl across her face. Her white jeans are covered in muddy paw prints visible from here. Neo is at her feet, begging for attention.

"Oh, fucking hell."

"What? Do you know her?"

"You could say that," Beau says, jumping from the wagon. "What the fuck are you doing here, Frankie?" he growls through clenched teeth.

"Who's Frankie?" Blake turns in her seat, looking first at me and then Mom. We both shrug.

"I don't know. But it doesn't sound good."

Life. Just when you think you've got it all figured out, the conniving bitch spins you around and tosses you right back on your ass. Oh, well. At least it's never boring.

ACKNOWLEDGEMENTS

A LOT of people helped make this book possible, and they deserve a proper thank you, so without further ado.

Amber, thank you for spamming me with GIFs daily and laughing at me when I really needed you to SUPPORT ME.

Fabiola, thank you for pushing me, thirty minutes at a time. I couldn't have done this without your motivation.

Dillon, thanks for letting me steal your name. (Psst. I stole your name.)

To my PLN sisters, I LOVE YOU and thank you so much for supporting me and pushing me to be a better human daily. Kirsten, Rebecca, Ruth, Amber, Victoria, Aria, Tarryn, Michelle, Holly H, Holly R, okay, okay now I'm just name dropping haha. You ladies have all been there for me in one way or another and your love is invaluable.

Thank you, husband, for waiting on me hand and foot, for driving the kids across the world, and for cooking dinner every night. You're the real MVP here, and without you, none of this would have been possible. I suppose I forgive you for throwing away my rug now. And to my wonderful children, thank you for existing.

And lastly, but certainly not least, THANK YOU, readers, for loving Calvin and Blake as much as I do!

ABOUT TINLEY

TINLEY BLAKE HAS SLEPT under the stars in Las Vegas, eaten dinner at midnight with French men who couldn't be trusted to keep their mouths on their food, and traveled across the countryside in stolen vehicles with worldwide drug men and lived to tell the tale.

She likes stories about family, loyalty, and extraordinary characters who struggle with basic human emotions while dealing with bigger than life problems. Tinley loves creating heroes who make you swoon, heroines who make you jealous, and the perfect Happily Ever After endings.

These days, you can find her writing in a sweet bungalow on the outskirts of Birmingham, Alabama, with her very own French man who is now her loving husband, their eight kids, two dogs, and one very confused cat named Goat.

Lastly, if you enjoyed this book, Tinley would be eternally grateful if you took the time to leave a review at Amazon and/or Goodreads. No spoilers, please ;-)

AUTHOR WORKS

THE WAY WE LOVED
THE WAY WE FOUGHT
LIAR LIAR: VOLUME ONE
SEXPLORATION
PARKER & ELIAS STORY
UNBROKEN
PACEY'S STORY

Printed in Great Britain
by Amazon